Books by Thom Collins

Anthem

Anthem of the Sea

Anthologies

Brothers in Arms

Single Titles

Closer by Morning

Anthem of the Sea

ISBN # 978-1-78686-177-1

©Copyright Thom Collins 2017

Cover Art by Posh Gosh ©Copyright 2017

Interior text design by Claire Siemaszkiewicz

Pride Publishing

Published in 2017 by Pride Publishing, Think Tank, Ruston Way, Lincoln, LN6 7FL, United Kingdom.

Pride Publishing is a subsidiary of Totally Entwined Group Limited.

Anthem

ANTHEM OF THE SEA

THOM COLLINS

Dedication

To Liam, as always.

Prologue

Sunday morning

The cry went out at one in the morning. An urgent call to the bridge.

"Man overboard! Starboard side. Turn. Turn. Turn."

Gale-force winds and fifty-foot waves had battered the ship since mid-afternoon and Captain Roman Rassimov was already on the bridge when the distress call came. A call dreaded by every captain at sea — man overboard. In twenty-seven years of service, this was his first. It had to be tonight, in this storm from hell.

Despite its three-hundred-fifty-meter length and one-hundred-sixty-seven-ton weight, the massive *Atlantic Anthem* turned swiftly in the violent ocean, aided by twin-propeller pods and four-bow thrusters. But it was no easy ride. In devastating winds and tremendous seas, the ship listed heavily on both sides as the swells tossed it as freely as a cork. Tables and chairs were overturned. Bottles and glasses smashed. Frightened passengers clung to any secure fixture to stop from going over.

Within minutes Captain Rassimov raised a call to other craft in the area, urging for help with the search and rescue.

By four o'clock, the area of low-pressure weather that had hounded the ship for fifteen hours pushed toward land and the sea conditions became more manageable. Spotlights were trained upon the waves and the captain deployed lifeboats to patrol the water level. A Norwegian cruise ship, coming back from a Mediterranean voyage, diverted from its course to join the hunt for the missing man.

As dawn broke around seven-thirty, a notice came back from one of the lifeboats. The man had been found.

A glimmer of hope flared in the captain's heart. "Is he alive?" he asked, offering a silent prayer.

The wait for the response was interminable.

"Negative, captain. There's nothing we can do. He's stone-cold dead."

Chapter One

The taxi collected Daniel Blake from the hotel on time. He liked that. Punctuality, efficiency and professionalism — three things he valued in all areas of his career. Be on time and be prepared — that had been his motto since he was fourteen years old. Fifteen years later, he continued to live by it.

He helped the driver load his gear into the trunk. There wasn't much of it. When on the road, he traveled light with just a medium-sized case, a holdall and a suit carrier. He'd arrived in Lisbon the previous morning, disembarking from a cruise ship, where he'd performed for two nights. His shirts would need washing and his suit pressing before his next show. There was plenty of time.

He gave the driver directions to his designated cruise terminal and climbed onto the back seat. Thankfully, the air conditioning was running. Though it was late October, the outside temperature remained in the mid-eighties and it wasn't even eleven o'clock. Last night he had heard some of the hotel staff complain about the weather turning cold, but for a boy like him, born and raised in the northeast of England, these climates were well above average. Back home, this would be a hot day in June or July.

It was a short drive to the port. Early in the day, but the streets were busy. Three massive cruise ships were anchored in the harbor, discharging thousands of eager tourists into the city. British, American, German, Japanese, they scurried through the streets, clutching backpacks and maps, keen to explore as much as they could of the historic Portuguese city in the few hours they had here.

Daniel smiled at their faces as they zipped by.

Lisbon, his last stop before home.

The car arrived at the port and within ten minutes Daniel stood beside the gangway with his luggage, waiting for the necessary security calls to be made that would allow him to board the ship. The enormous vessel towered above him, casting a huge shadow across the dock. The *Atlantic* was one of the biggest and most spectacular cruise ships in the world.

There were a lot of criticisms for super ships such as this. He'd heard them described as floating shopping malls, grotesque monstrosities and budget hotels at sea, but for Daniel there was something quite majestic about the craft and its design, to say nothing of the engineering that went into the construction of such a huge vessel.

"Those things are so top heavy," a jobbing magician once had told him in a bar. "I hear they roll right over in high seas."

Daniel had laughed at the man's ignorance. "And when did you last hear of that happening?"

The man had floundered. "I'm just saying that something so uneven can't be safe, can it? You won't ever catch me on one of them things. Mug's game, isn't it?"

"It's your loss," Daniel had told him cheerily. He felt safer at sea, even in the roughest weather, than he ever had on a plane. Motorways too. It might not be the quickest, but without a doubt it was the most luxurious and extravagant way to travel. He loved being at sea.

Waiting for the security guy to return with his passport, Daniel realized he'd drawn some attention.

A slow stream of passengers was returning to the ship. They couldn't have seen much of Lisbon, coming back already. Among them was an English family. While the parents lit cigarettes before joining the embarkation queue, the daughter, who looked around fourteen, stared directly at him.

"Hi." He smiled. "Good day out?"

The girl was plump and pretty with wavy brown hair that fell around her shoulders. She wore a sweet, flowery sundress and red Converse shoes. She blushed as she realized she'd been caught gawking.

"Are you...? Oh, my God, you are, aren't you? You're Daniel Blake."

He raised his hands in mock surrender. "Guilty as charged. Don't shoot me."

The girl nervously stepped forward, looking at him with wide, hazel eyes. "What are you doing here?"

"I'm waiting to join the ship. I'm performing on board."

Her jaw fell. "The *Anthem*? You're coming on the *Anthem*?"

He nodded. He didn't mind being recognized like this. Daniel was famous enough in the UK, but not so much that it ever became an inconvenience. His fame came from a TV talent show. The public had made him and he appreciated all the support he got.

"Oh my God." The girl's face became highly animated. *"Mam! Dad!* Come here. Oh my God, you won't believe it. *Daniel Blake.* It's actually him."

Her bemused parents stubbed out their cigarettes and came over. They were an attractive-looking couple of around forty. The girl looked a lot like her father.

"I hope she's not bothering you," the dad said, looking cautiously between Daniel and his daughter.

"Not a bit," Daniel assured him. "It's a pleasure."

"Daniel is going to be singing on the ship. Can you believe it? How cool is that?" She grinned a mile wide.

"Starting tomorrow," he said. "Make certain you get yourselves a great seat down front. I can use all the support I can get."

"I will, I will. I voted for you every week on *The One*. You were my favorite from the start."

"So it's you I need to thank for winning. What's your name, sweetie?"

"Julieann."

"Well, thank you, Julieann. Your votes changed my life."

The girl blushed violently.

The security officer came back to escort Daniel onto the ship. Before boarding, he posed for photographs with Julieann and her family.

"The girls at school will have a fit when they see these on Instagram," Julieann said proudly as they took a selfie together.

"See you at the shows," Daniel said as he walked on board. "And don't forget—front row. Be there. I'll look out for you."

"We'll definitely be there."

Once on board, he passed his luggage through the security scanner and was equipped with his sea pass ID, the plastic card that would enable him to move around the ship, access his accommodation and run a tab in the bars and shops. He was greeted on the far side of security by a young woman in a blue shirt and khaki shorts. Her soft blonde hair was tied back from her round, attractive face. She was vaguely familiar from his engagement earlier in the season. He checked her name badge to refresh his memory. Belle Hodges, entertainment crew, from South Australia.

"Hi," Belle said cheerily. "It's wonderful to have you back on board."

She extended her hand and he shook it. "It's great to be back. Honestly, I've been looking forward to this since I left in May. How has your maiden season gone?"

"Over too quickly and totally ace. I can't believe it's been that long since you were here. Yikes, the time has flown. Let me give you a hand with your stuff."

"That's okay. I can manage. Just point me in the right direction and I'll find my way."

Ignoring his protests, Belle took up the suit carrier.

"You're in real luck," she said. "You've been allocated a large stateroom on one of the passenger decks. Balcony and all."

"You're joking? Wow. Am I sharing with the house band or a football team?"

Belle giggled, wrinkling her nose. "Silly. You've got the whole place to yourself."

"Seriously? What gives? I never get accommodation like that."

Belle looked around cautiously and lowered her voice. "We had a family thrown off the ship in Gran Canaria so you've got their room. They caused a fight in the martini bar and punched an officer who tried to intervene. Captain Rassimov put them off at the next port. No second chances."

"Good to know we're in such firm hands."

"Captain Rassimov is the best," Belle gushed.

Daniel didn't doubt it. He'd met the dashing captain on his last trip. Tall, dark, handsome and extremely charismatic, he sent hearts beating fast among the passengers and crew. If he wasn't so straight, Daniel would fancy him too. Rassimov was the perfect man to master such a grand vessel.

Launched in May, with a rumored cost of over one-point-five billion, the *Atlantic Anthem* was coming to the end of its inaugural European season. It was the newest and biggest vessel in the Royal Atlantic fleet. Daniel had spent two nights on board when he'd performed a headline set on the maiden voyage. He'd worked for cruise companies all over the world, but he couldn't fail to be impressed by the *Anthem*. It was billed as the ship with everything. From his own experience that was certainly true.

As he walked through the decks with Belle, his sense of excitement increased. The interior was truly splendid. Not a penny had been spared, from the lush carpets to the paintings and sculptures that graced every deck. Before coming on board, he'd read all the specs — about the spa and fitness center, two swimming pools and a solarium, the Royal Theater with nine-hundred-sixty seats, the bars — eight of them across the ship — the main dining room plus three specialty restaurants and a twenty-four-hour café. Several public entertainment areas were situated on Decks Four and Five around a jaw-dropping central staircase.

Knowing all of that in advance, he still had been blown away when he'd came upon the ship for the first time. And he felt it now, all over again.

Only the most jaded, spoiled and hard-to-please traveler could fail to be inspired by the *Anthem*.

They rode one of the glass elevators to the tenth floor where Belle led him down a long corridor to his stateroom in the forward section of the ship.

"Last time, I had an interior cabin in the crew quarters." He laughed.

"Yep, that's where they like to cram us in. But now you've got this."

Daniel swiped his sea pass card to enter the room. A major step up from crew class, the room was bright and contemporary, to the standard of any good hotel. He had an enormous double bed all to himself and a sitting area with a long, cream leather sofa. There was a dressing table, minibar, TV, private bathroom and balcony.

"I hope I don't get lost in here," he joked, dumping his luggage by the wardrobe.

"As long as you're on stage for your shows tomorrow night, no one will mind what you get up to in here," Belle said.

"You can put your mind at ease on that count," he said. "I've been performing since I was fourteen and I've never missed a show in my life."

Belle left him to settle in. Daniel unpacked his clothes first and filled a plastic bag with stuff that needed washing immediately—shirts, socks and underwear. Another great thing about working on a luxury cruise liner—everything was to hand. If he left the bag out today, all the items would be washed, ironed and returned by tomorrow.

He went into the bathroom next, laying out his razor, toothbrush and skincare products. He brought everything with him when he traveled. Though he wasn't particularly vain, it was important to look good in public.

He didn't have to worry. At twenty-nine years old—five

months shy of thirty—he was in prime condition. He'd never looked better. For years he used to hate the way he looked. Everything about him had been out of proportion, especially his face. Eyes, teeth, nose, chin, they were always too big. But throughout his twenties, the rest of his body had caught up. He'd filled out and gained muscle and his face, which had seemed so awkward in his teens, had developed an extraordinary handsomeness. He had a strong jaw with a cowboy cleft, while his mouth was wide and masculine. With sky-blue eyes and thick brown hair, he had become a good-looking man. Very good-looking.

His confidence hadn't grown to match his looks. A part of him would always be that skinny, peculiar kid. But only he could see it.

Finally unpacked, he relaxed and walked onto the balcony. He had a great view of the city and the people below, streaming like ants around the port terminals. Daniel took a moment to enjoy it all. He loved just about every part of the cruise experience.

Every ship, every voyage, was a new adventure.

The *Atlantic Anthem* promised a greater adventure than any other.

He couldn't wait to get started.

Chapter Two

Elijah Mann tried to ignore Vladislav Kolodin's heated fingers as they jerked persistently on his cock. The Russian dancer had been going at it for over ten minutes and it took a tremendous effort to keep his eyes shut and his breathing under control. Why was he here? Elijah had expected the Russian to go back to his own cabin at some point during the night but no, here he was, throttling the life out of Elijah's morning wood, determined to have his share.

"Stop pretending to be asleep," Vladislav said impatiently. "No one can sleep through this."

Doubtlessly true.

"I'm tired," Elijah grumbled as Vladislav gripped him tighter. Reluctantly he opened his eyes. "Knock it off, will you?"

"That's what I'm trying to do."

The Russian threw the bed clothes from their naked bodies and went down on Elijah's dick, sucking him deep into his hot mouth.

What the hell. Give him what he wants. Maybe it'll get rid of him. Some guys would kill for such a problem. Elijah widened his legs and succumbed to Vladislav's hungry lips, arching his back from the bed.

A double bed in a large stateroom. Now *that* was something to savor. As a jobbing comedian, Elijah often found himself consigned to crew quarters when he worked on cruise ships. But thanks to Helen McDonald, cruise director on the amazing *Atlantic Anthem*, he'd been allocated one of the larger staterooms all to himself. No wonder Vladislav was reluctant to go back to his own cabin, a basic interior room with bunk beds he would share with one of the other guys in the ship's company. It would be worth the effort of a blow job to spend the night in a decent bed.

How had it come to this?

Elijah had been introduced to the Russian late the previous night. He'd been having a drink with a group of staff from the entertainment team when Vladislav had sidled up and introduced himself as one of the dancers. He wasn't even Elijah's type. With perfectly styled blond hair and glassy blue eyes, he had golden skin and a clear complexion. The kind of good looks found in glossy magazines advertising expensive aftershave. A clean-cut face without a trace of character. Bland, bland, bland. He'd never been interested in those plucked and oiled models with their ultra-defined abs and hard, shapeless arses but Vladislav had the image nailed.

It had been a huge surprise at the end of the night to find himself pressed against a wall with Vladislav's tongue thrust deep in his mouth and his hard cock grinding against his thigh. Even worse, he'd responded to it and tumbled into bed with the insistent dancer.

He'd put up no resistance.

Unlike Vladislav, Elijah did not have a six-pack. He had neither the time nor the desire to cultivate one. He was in good shape with wide shoulders, a nice, hairy chest and a fairly flat stomach. He was confident in his body. But going to bed with a man like Vladislav, someone so incredibly ripped, made him self-conscious. Not just because of his six-pack or rock-hard thighs — it was the veins that popped on his arms and abdomen. He was a physically intimidating sight.

Still, there was nothing intimidating about the sex.

Vladislav was a terrible lover. The foreplay had been clumsy and rough. For the main event, he'd rolled over, stuck his butt in the air and begged Elijah to fuck him. Which he had. And it had been *so* boring. He seemed to think he was so physically beautiful, all he had to do was lie

15

there and give his lover the honor of screwing him. Elijah liked men who were his equal in the sack, who gave as good as they got, but Vladislav offered nothing.

It seemed that as far as Vlad was concerned, giving up his butt was more than enough.

It had turned into the most tiresome one-night stand of Elijah's life. So why were they going through the motions again?

Vladislav climbed on top of him, wielding a condom. He tore into the wrapper and rolled the rubber over Elijah's cock, murmuring delight at the size and thickness of him. The Russian had a big cock of his own, befitting his porn-star looks, but seemed to have no urge to use it. Probably just as well. If his technique as a top was as deficient as his skills as a bottom, it would likely result in one very painful fuck.

Better we stick to our established roles, Elijah thought.

Vladislav slathered his dick with lube and impaled himself upon it.

"Yes," he hissed, taking it all the way.

Lying back, head propped on pillows, Elijah allowed himself to be ridden. Surely there must be something wrong with him, because this smooth, granite body grinding away on top failed to excite him in any way. His cock stayed hard throughout—things hadn't gotten *that* bad—but he didn't feel the slightest connection to the man on top of him.

Vladislav's shaved balls and cock smacked against Elijah's belly. He closed his eyes and tweaked his nipples as his hips jerked up and down. His golden skin glistened with sweat. He released the grip on his tit and seized his cock, tugging furiously. He exposed his teeth, screwed up his face and splattered Elijah's chest with his hot load.

"Whoa," the Russian said as he shuddered through the end of his orgasm. Then he lifted off and dashed to the bathroom, slamming the door behind him.

"I guess we're done," Elijah said, grabbing a wad of tissues and using them to pull the slimy condom off his cock. "You've been a great audience. Thank you and good night."

He rolled off the bed and drew on a pair of shorts. Their clothes were spread all over the room. He had really lost it last night, just a drunken, horny fool.

He stepped over the debris and opened the curtains. Elijah smiled. The balcony was a real bonus. Since he'd joined the ship in Tenerife two days earlier, it had been more like a holiday than a job. He'd sat on the balcony both evenings and had watched the sun set over the Atlantic Ocean. It didn't get much better than that. Elijah enjoyed solitude.

Today they were docked in Lisbon.

Elijah opened the sliding door and stepped onto the balcony. *What a beautiful morning.* Late October and the sun was unusually warm on his bare skin. He rubbed his eyes and blinked, bringing the sprawling city into view, with its imbalance of historic old buildings and modern eyesores. He'd stayed here several times before. The port was a key hop on-hop off point for cruise entertainers, with most of the major lines operating itineraries that called here regularly. He liked a lot of things about Lisbon. It was a busy, bustling, noisy city with so much going on, so many things to do and see.

Vladislav came out of the bathroom. Elijah, desperate for a piss, hurried in after him and relieved himself. His hard-on had dwindled and he avoided flooding the room with urine.

He washed his hands and brushed damp fingers through his wild blue-black hair. It stuck up at a million different angles. He added more water and flattened it into something less alarming.

Vladislav had dressed in black skinny jeans and a T-shirt when he returned to the bedroom. He held a black sock in one hand while searching the floor for its partner.

Now this was awkward. What to say? There was clearly *nothing* going on between them. They had nothing in common apart from working on the ship and sharing a night of mediocre sex. The start of a great romance, it certainly wasn't.

Elijah spotted the stray sock down the side of the bed and handed it to the dancer.

"Are you doing much today?" he asked brightly, knowing how cheesy the smile he had fixed on his face must look. "Going into town? Shopping?"

"No. I have work. It's *Groovy Time* tonight. We must rehearse."

"*Groovy Time*?"

"Seventies disco on Deck Fifteen. Terrible show but lots of hard work. The passengers like it."

"Oh, that sounds…fun. Maybe I'll check it out after my show."

Vladislav pulled on his shoes. "Yes," he said without looking at him. "I think *you* will like it. Your kind of music."

Oh! How old does he think I am?

"I'm thirty-three," Elijah blurted.

Smiling wryly, the Russian stood. "Okay. You mustn't tell anyone that I was with you last night. The company doesn't look fondly on us getting together like this."

"I thought those rules only applied to screwing the passengers."

Vladislav grimaced. "They are strict about all behavior. Besides, this is a passenger room on one of the passenger decks. I must not have been seen here. Goodbye."

Without a parting kiss or even a hand shake Vladislav headed to the door. He opened it a fraction, pressing his ear to the crack, then, apparently satisfied, he slipped into the corridor and closed the door behind him.

What a strange boy. However drunk he got on the rest of the voyage, he must never let that happen again.

Elijah was no stranger to one-night stands. He got his fair share of offers and found it hard to say no. Being over six foot two with black hair and a long, straight nose and wide mouth, he drew plenty of attention. The definition of tall, dark and handsome. His mixed heritage—half Greek, half

English — gave his skin a naturally bronzed and swarthy tone. It had been noted by more than one comedy critic that Elijah was 'too good-looking to be really funny'. *Talk about back-handed compliments.*

His all-round good looks meant he was never short of a bedroom companion. When sexy guys threw themselves at him, it would be rude to reject them and his mother had raised him to always be polite. But the appeal of sleeping around had worn off. Vladislav was not the first casual fuck to leave him underwhelmed and dissatisfied.

Maybe he'd grown out of it. He was thirty-three after all. Time to grow up and find a real man to have a relationship with. *Yeah, right, as if that's any easier.*

Whatever he decided, it was time to cool things down. Stop shagging around like an uncontrollable slut with every half-hot man he met. Quality over quantity. He could surely use some of that.

Elijah grabbed his phone and dialed his friend Anouska, another dancer in the ship's company.

"Hey, lover boy," she answered straight away. "Is big, bad Vlad still with you?"

So much for Vladislav's secret. "How come you know about that already?"

"Are you kidding?" Anouska laughed. "Everybody knows. We all saw you last night. Chewing each other's faces off in the mess room is not exactly discreet."

"He just left. He asked me to keep quiet about the whole thing."

"Silly boy. He's been on board long enough to know there are no secrets between crew."

"Will he get in trouble?"

"Doubt it. You're working here, not a paying guest. Most people are so horny on board these things by the end of the season everyone has had sex with everyone else. I got it on with one of the gays in Guest Relations last week. He'd already been through all the available guys and he was open to something new — *moi*."

19

"That's what I love about you," Elijah said. "You never let an opportunity pass you by. How about breakfast? Want to go ashore and get something?"

"Sorry. I don't have time today. We've got rehearsals all afternoon."

"*Groovy Time?*"

"You got it." Anouska laughed. "I can spare an hour now. How about Cafe24? Ten minutes?"

"See you there," he said and hung up.

After a very quick shower, Elijah combed his damp hair, put on clean chinos and a navy T-shirt and took the lift to Deck Sixteen. As he made his way toward the twenty-four-hour café, he caught a couple of curious glances from passengers. He'd yet to perform his headline show — that was not until this evening — but he usually drew a few eager eyes and 'don't I know you?' comments due to his appearances on UK television. In no way could he be called famous, but his face wasn't entirely unfamiliar to people.

He smiled happily at those who stared and moved briskly on before they had time to recognize him.

Anouska Frost waited at the entrance to the café. Devoid of makeup, dressed in a baggy T-shirt and leggings, with her long red hair in a plain ponytail, she was quite unrecognizable as the glamourous showgirl she portrayed in ship's big production shows. She was slender and petite. Elijah had to stoop to plant a welcome kiss on her freckled cheek.

"I passed Vlad on the way up," she said. "Taking the walk of shame back to his cabin. An all-nighter, eh?"

"I think he loves me for my double bed," Elijah quipped.

"Can't blame him for that. Vlad bunks with one of the musicians. A real beer and curry fan, if you know what I'm saying. The stink from their toilet sometimes poisons the entire corridor."

"Nice. I won't let anyone ever tell me that life on board a cruise ship isn't twenty-four-hour glamour."

"Glamour's nothing but a façade. You know that. Come

on, let's eat. I'm starving and I've got a lot to do today."

Cafe24 was a huge buffet restaurant at the very top of the ship. Floor-to-ceiling windows presented some of the very best ocean views but few people came here to appreciate the scenery. The café offered an enormous array of food every hour of the day and night. Cuisine from all over the world that catered to every taste from healthy to decadent. Meats, salads, seafood, stews, stir-fries, cakes, breads, fruit, pizzas, hotdogs, breakfast, lunch and dinner. Whatever time of day, whatever you were looking for, you would find it here.

Most cruise ships offered some variation on the twenty-four-hour buffet. Elijah went out of his way to avoid them. He wasn't the greatest fan of self-service dining. It brought out the worst in people — the most gluttonous, greedy part of their nature — himself included. Why take one muffin when a person could fill their plate with three? Don't have two sausages, take five. The waste produced from these places was outrageous as half-eaten plates were scraped into the rubbish bin.

As ever, the café was heaving when they arrived. There were no quiet periods at an all-you-can-eat buffet. Even today, with the ship in port and many of the passengers ashore, it was packed. They helped themselves to orange juice and set about finding a seat. Never easy, but they secured a table between a colossal British family and a striking young Spanish couple.

Elijah steeled himself. "Okay, let's do this."

The hordes were swarming around the hot breakfast counter, so he took a plate and headed for the less crowded continental section. He helped himself to some cured meat, tomatoes, manchego cheese, smoked mackerel and a slice of olive bread. Not bad. Not too excessive.

He retreated to the relative calm of their table and narrowly avoiding being knocked over by a large lady in an orange kaftan who wasn't looking where she was going. Anouska returned a few moments later with a mountain of food. Sausages, bacon, grilled tomatoes, mushrooms, scrambled and fried eggs, baked beans, hash browns and black pudding. On a separate plate, she carried four slices of toasted white bread.

"You did well," Elijah laughed. "To get all that and make it out alive."

"Practice," she said, dunking her toast straight into an egg yolk. "After all these years, I'm accustomed to the ways of the sea. When it comes to a buffet, I can take anyone on and win."

He looked at her enormous plate and then his own simple breakfast. It was tiny in comparison. And still, he wasn't jealous.

"So how was the beautiful Russian?" she asked as her knife and fork worked overtime.

"I never kiss and tell," he replied. "And I'm not about to start."

"Spoilsport. What's the point of a gossipy breakfast if you're not going to gossip?"

"I'm an honorable gentleman," he said. "Not many of us around but here I am. What about Vlad? Am I just another notch on a very long bedpost?"

"I wouldn't have thought so. Vlad's no virgin but he doesn't appear to put it about like the rest of the chorus boys. If he does, then he's discreet about it. Some of those guys, my God, they're in the wrong profession. If they weren't so intent on giving it all away, they would make a fortune on their backs."

Elijah laughed. Anouska was always good company. They'd met five years earlier on a TV variety show. She'd been a backing dancer for a flamboyant male singer. Elijah had had three minutes of stand-up between a dancing dog and a Romanian sword swallower. They had gotten to chatting while hanging around during rehearsals. Anouska had a brazen sense of humor and a line in dirty anecdotes. She'd had him in stitches with tales of a tour she'd once done with John Barrowman. They'd hit it off straight away and when she'd approached him on Facebook a few days later, they'd quickly became good friends. When work had run dry on his regular comedy circuits, Anouska had suggested he take his act to sea.

"Decent comedians are like gold dust in this line. Believe me, babe, they'll be falling over themselves to book you."

She wasn't wrong. He'd barely been home in six months, taking his act all over Europe on a variety of ships. The audiences were different from what he was used to and he had to tone down his material considerably for the family crowd, but he didn't regret his decision. Not for a moment. If nothing came along in the meantime, he would happily do it all again next year.

"Are you all set for tonight?" Anouska asked, shoveling another forkful into her mouth. If she didn't burn so much energy through her dancing, she'd be the size of a house — a bigger-than-average house.

"Pretty much," he said. "I've got a run-through on the main stage this afternoon. There are a couple of new jokes I want to try out, but other than that I'm good to go."

"Are you finished after that?"

"Just about. Helen asked me to do a fifteen-minute slot in the finale on the last night of the cruise, but after my headline shows tonight, I'm pretty much done and can relax."

As with most cruise ships, the *Atlantic Anthem* offered an early and a late sitting option for dinner. To ensure all guests got the opportunity to see the entertainment, the headliners performed the same show twice each evening. Tonight, he was due to go on at eight-thirty and ten-thirty, performing for an hour each time.

"When will you be back?" she asked. "On the ship, I mean."

"Not until next year." This was his final booking of the season. At the end of the voyage, the ship would sail to North America to operate a winter sun itinerary around the Caribbean. While some of the entertainment crew would stay on board, the work dried up for European guest entertainers like Elijah, when they were rightly bumped in favor of local talent.

"Bitten by the bug?" she asked.

"I'll say. A cushy number like this. Decent money, headline spots, a chance to see the world. If anything, it bothers me that I could take it all for granted. Though I'm sure a winter back in the UK, staying in travel lodges and hoping to land a spot on *Have I Got News For You* will batter any complacency out of me."

"*Have I Got News For You* will be lucky to have you. A bit like Vladislav was, eh?"

"FYI—Vlad didn't have me."

Anouska chuckled. "I knew I'd get something out of you. *Gentleman* indeed."

Chapter Three

"Daniel, my love, it's sooo good to see you."

Helen McDonald tottered across the stage in a pair of impossibly high-heeled shoes. She came down the front stairs and dashed up the center aisle of the auditorium to receive him with open arms. She smothered him in a friendly embrace and clouds of sweet perfume. Her reception was real and welcoming. Fifty-four years old, tall and tan, she was never seen with an immaculately bleached hair out of place.

There were a lot of corporate-minded cruise directors in the business, going through the motions, delivering their scripted patter with the dead-eyed gaze of a shark. Helen was not one of them.

"It's good to be back." Daniel laughed, returning the hug. "Thanks for having me."

"If I had my way, you'd be on every cruise on my itinerary. You know I mean that. Say the word and I'll draw up the contract."

"Don't tempt me, please. I absolutely love this ship. I'm jealous — you get to live on this thing. Not like work at all, eh?"

She chuckled. "Oh, it's work all right. Have no doubt about that, but it's the best job in the world." She stepped back and held him at arm's length. "Let me look at you. You've lost weight, love. They've not been looking after you on those other ships. Get yourself up to Cafe24 and fill your boots before you get too skinny."

"I've no doubt I'll gain a few pounds between here and England."

"That's what cruising is all about."

Daniel turned to take in the huge art déco theater. It was sleek, sexy, elegant and vast. Looking at the rows of empty seats, he experienced a thrill deep in his core, remembering the excitement of a full house. Performing on the maiden voyage was one of the best nights he'd had on stage. The excitement had been palpable. Audience, crew, performers — everyone felt it. A brand-new ship, beginning her journey with so many adventures ahead.

It was an honor to be back and closing the season.

They headed up the steps to the stage. A couple of technicians were tinkering with one of the moveable lighting rigs. The stage itself was enormous, bigger than a lot of the city center theaters he'd performed in.

"What have the crowds been like?"

"Can't complain," Helen said. "Some nights are better than others. It's not always easy to draw them in for a juggler or a magician but comedians and singers have been going down well. We've got a comedian on tonight. And there's already a buzz among the passengers about your shows this weekend. You've got nothing to worry about. You'll have three full houses, that's a certainty."

"I hope so." There was no room for complacency. Cruise ship audiences were notoriously difficult beasts. Unlike an ordinary tour, none of the passengers had paid specifically to see him. They could take or leave the entertainment as it suited them. Mostly he'd been lucky, though he'd recently played on a ship geared toward an older cliental. His early show had gone down well enough, but the theater was sparsely populated for his late set. By eleven p.m. most nights the ship was desolate.

"We've got a good crowd on board this cruise," Helen said. "They're all up for a party. We've been rocking till two most mornings. So come on, love, tell me what we've got to look forward to."

"Okay, with the shows tomorrow night, I will stick with the crowd pleasers — entertainment all the way. Some big pop numbers, a handful of show tunes. Give them all a party."

"Fantastic," Helen declared, throwing up her hands. "Give 'em some Bublé, they love that."

"I don't do Bublé, Helen. You know that."

"What? Still? Everyone does Bublé, love."

"Exactly." His eyes twinkled but his voice stayed firm. "*Everyone*. I'm sure your guests have heard more than enough for one cruise."

She chuckled. "You're a wicked boy. All right, no Bublé. The old dears will be devastated but I'll give you that. No Bublé. What about your matinee?"

"Something a little varied. More personal. Songs that have significant meaning to me and stories attached that I can share with the audience. I tested it on my last tour and it went down really well, so I've expanded it to an hour for your matinee."

"That sounds wonderful. I can't wait to see it. The band is available for rehearsals tomorrow afternoon. Does that sound all right or do you want more time?"

"Nah. Your guys know what they're doing. We'll be up to speed in a couple of hours."

"You're a man of leisure today then. The ship's all yours. Get out there and enjoy it."

A door opened at the back of the auditorium. They both turned to look. A tall figure came down the central aisle, making for the stage. Helen shielded her eyes against the lights.

"Ah, it's Elijah. Tonight's headliner. A brilliant comedian. You must catch his show. You'll love him."

Hello, Elijah.

From halfway across the theater, in the dim light, he already liked what he saw. Black hair, broad shoulders, dark, sun-kissed skin. Daniel's pulse raced. This guy was beautiful.

The man came down to the front, passed before the stage and mounted the steps to meet them. Daniel's heart suddenly beat a lot faster as he came face to with the best-looking man he'd ever seen.

Elijah knew exactly who Daniel was the moment he saw him. Someone would have to be living on the moon for the last six years to not recognize him. He'd become a household name since winning that Saturday night singing competition *The One*. Not as famous as Will Young or Olly Murs — nobody saw *them* performing on cruise ships — but in the field of disposable TV talent, Daniel had been resilient. His star burned brighter than most of his contemporaries.

Elijah had always liked what he'd seen of Daniel. He was a knock-out singer and came across as warm and personable on TV. And definitely easy on the eye. But when it came to looks the TV did him a disservice. In the flesh, he was much more handsome — an absolute stunner.

It was hard not to stare. He was *that* good-looking.

Elijah tried to keep his cool and struggled.

"Hi," he said, thrusting forth his hand. "Elijah Mann. I'm so pleased to meet you."

Daniel smiled, so wide and bright it illuminated the stage like a spotlight. "Oh my God," he said, vigorously pumping Elijah's hand. "When Helen said there was a comedian on tonight, I didn't think it would be you. Elijah Mann from *Shades of England*. I love you guys."

Helen grinned like a proud mother. "Do you know each other already?"

"No," Daniel said, blue eyes sparkling. "I'm a fan, that's all. *Shades of England* is one of my favorite shows. When I toured the UK, me and the band used to watch episodes back to back on the bus between venues. It was so funny. We'd watch them again and again and it never got tired."

Shades of England had started life as a successful radio comedy that Elijah co-wrote and acted in with fellow comedians Sonny Chamberlain and Ross Benson. It had run for three series on Radio 4 before being commissioned as a TV series on BBC3. Strong reviews had made comparisons to *Little Britain* and *The League of Gentlemen* and the show had developed a substantial cult following but it had failed to win much of an audience. It had been canceled at the end of its first run.

Still, it was nice of Daniel to say he liked it. He met so many people with a vague awareness that they'd seen him in something without knowing what.

He stared at Daniel's face again. *Shit, he's sooo handsome.* Those blue eyes were mesmerizing. And that cleft jaw — he was like the hero in a spaghetti western, only much better looking.

Thankfully, Helen stepped in and broke the spell. "It's just as well you get along. I want you both to do a spot in Saturday night's finale. It's the last show of the cruise — the season in fact — and I want it to be something out of this world. Are you both in for that?"

"Absolutely," Elijah said.

"Count me in." Daniel smiled.

Good Lord, that smile.

Elijah couldn't remember when he'd ever been smitten by someone as instantly as this. Was it love at first sight or just all-consuming lust? Both? Something was already stirring in his underpants. Daniel's good looks cast a powerful spell and he'd fallen directly under its influence.

"So, you're doing your show tonight?" Daniel asked, looking him straight in the eye.

"I am," he said, pulling himself together. "Yes, that's why I'm here, actually. I wanted to walk through the material with the lighting guys. Get a feel for the stage and all that."

"Of course," Helen said. "Then we'll leave you to it." She linked arms with Daniel and guided him to the wings.

"I'm looking forward to seeing your show," Daniel said as Helen shuffled him away.

"Likewise."

Elijah watched him go. Dear God, the rear view was as stunning as the front. He had wide shoulders which tapered to a compact waist and — *holy shit* — that arse. Bootilicious.

Every part of him was perfect.

Impossible. No one could be *that* beautiful. Maybe he had a freakishly small penis or an unsightly skin condition that blighted his whole torso. Maybe he was cruel to animals and children and vile to his mother. Except none of that could be true. He was indeed flawless.

Just as he withdrew into the wings, Daniel glanced back and smiled. It looked kind of shy, almost vulnerable. Something surged inside Elijah.

"Just a second," he called after Daniel. He couldn't let him go as easily as this. Something had just happened between them. Whatever it was, he had to act on it. "I'll be done here in an hour. Do you fancy getting together for a coffee? Maybe even a light lunch."

There, he'd said it. Emboldened, the words poured out of him.

Daniel's eyes were as bright as his smile. Without hesitation he said, "Love to."

Something flipped. Elijah's pulse rate increased. "How about one o'clock? There's a bar on the top deck, toward the stern. They do food as well as drinks."

"I know it," Daniel said. "I'll see you there."

Then he was gone, leaving Elijah breathless. Awestruck. *What the hell just happened?*

Following their introduction, Elijah found it hard to concentrate on what he had to do. Daniel was something else. As he tried to turn his mind toward that evening's show, it kept wandering to the sexy singer.

Pull yourself together man, you're a professional, not a giddy teenager. He dragged himself back to the moment and spoke to the one of the lighting guys about the format of his show, giving him a rough overview of how he would move about the stage and where he wanted the lights.

They came up with a few prearranged signals between them. The main content of the show was fixed, but comedy was a fluid beast and its success depended wholly on the audience. Some things worked better than others and he had to judge the reaction constantly throughout the show, knowing when to move on when something fell flat or elaborating when the crowd was on his side. He never performed the exact same show more than once.

He couldn't go too risqué tonight. Not with the cruise ship crowd. His contract forbade anything too mucky, but there was still a lot of fun to be had, playing off the crowd. A little innuendo went a long way with a family audience.

At the end of the rehearsal he was joined by the Anthem Orchestra. They had fifteen minutes to spare before their next gig to run through the song he would use to close the show. A comedy number, heavy on words which he spoke rather than sung for the most part. He knew his own strengths and singing wasn't one of them, but he had learned it inside out and it took only two runs through for the musicians to pick up their parts.

"Fantastic, guys. Great job."

They were professionals, used to receiving new music at short notice. His funny little song posed no problem to them.

Elijah left the theater by the main entrance. Lunch time and the ship was a lot livelier than before. They weren't expected to depart until five o'clock but a lot of the guests had returned from their day out in Lisbon. Along the main promenade, the bars and cafes were filling up. He smiled cheerfully at strangers as he passed. It was vital to keep up a happy exterior in the public areas of the ship. He wasn't strictly a member of staff but he felt obliged to adhere to the rules.

It was in a performer's best interest to keep the passengers happy. A few disgruntled comments on the customer satisfaction survey at the end the cruise could have a grossly negative effect on any further contracts. He knew of one comedian who'd been blacklisted by all the major companies after getting drunk in a public bar and calling an American passenger *a fat pant-suited cunt*.

It was just a joke, the man protested later, but no one had

laughed, least of all him. His cruise ship career had died overnight.

Elijah was in no position to provoke the guests. He needed jobs like this. *Shades of England* might have enjoyed a second lease of life on Daniel Blake's tour bus but it was four long years since the BBC had canceled the show.

Elijah headed straight for his stateroom. He was on a mission. He had twenty minutes to spare until his meeting with Daniel. Enough time to freshen up and brush his teeth. His nerves were beginning to twitch. Almost as if he was going on a date. That was stupid. They were going for coffee. It wasn't a date.

However much he wished it was.

* * * *

The early afternoon sun was fierce but a refreshing breeze blew across the upper decks of the ship. At sixteen-stories high, the *Atlantic Anthem* was taller than most of the buildings in the city beyond. Daniel took the forward elevator all the way to the top and walked the full length of the vessel to reach the bar in the stern.

His earlier stay on board had been too brief, and he wanted to spend time today getting acquainted with the ship.

He crossed through the massive solarium, with two indoor pools and four Jacuzzis. It was quiet at that time of day, with an ample supply of empty beds. He might come back later and grab a couple of hours with his Kindle and some tunes. Technically, this was his day off. His time was his own, so he might as well enjoy it while he could. With a baseball cap pulled low and a pair of shades, he was unlikely to be recognized.

The main pool deck was busier than the solarium. People swam and sunbathed, enjoying the sun while it lasted. They would all be back in England and the bracing autumn weather soon enough.

Daniel reached the bar with five minutes to spare. Exactly how he liked it. He didn't go in for being fashionably late or any of that shit. It wasn't fashionable — it was rude. *Get there on time if not before.* It was a simple courtesy. He found a table in the shade with a good view of the sprawling city beneath.

He realized for the first time that his heart was beating faster than normal. Elijah had asked to meet him for coffee, maybe lunch. They were two solitary travelers, entertainers getting to know each other, staving off the loneliness that was a fact of life for people who spent their lives away from home. It was no big deal. It was lunch, not a date. *A pity.*

There had been a spark between them when they'd met. Daniel was sure he hadn't imagined it. And it wasn't just one-sided either. His gaydar was seldom that wrong.

He'd always fancied Elijah. *Shades of England* was a funny show, but that wasn't the reason he liked it so much. Elijah Mann was a real hunk and hilarious with it. A rare combination. He was a brilliant impressionist and could hit a joke or one-liner out of the park.

Daniel had no idea whether Elijah was gay or not. *You still don't,* he reminded himself. But Elijah had called after him and asked to meet, and there had been something in his eyes when they'd faced each other on the stage. *A trick of the light? Wishful thinking?* What did it matter? He was about to have coffee with a handsome and funny man. If that was all it amounted to, then he would still do all right.

Elijah arrived exactly on time. Daniel stood to meet him, already smiling. Struck again by how good-looking he was. Elijah gripped his hand, shook it firmly and put another enthusiastic hand on Daniel's biceps. A friendly gesture, but the contact was filled with possibility.

"Thanks for coming," Elijah said, taking the chair next to Daniel rather than opposite.

"No, thanks for asking me," Daniel said. "I rarely get the chance to socialize when playing on a ship. The on-board crew work around the clock. It's hard to pin them down, even for a quick coffee."

"I know what you mean. My friend, Anouska, is a dancer on here. She never stops."

He had changed his shirt, Daniel noticed. It was pale blue and short-sleeved and fitted the masculine lines of his torso. His forearms were strong and swathed in silky brown hair. The same darkness showed in the open neck of his shirt. Daniel pulled focus back to Elijah's face.

"How did your rehearsal go?" he asked.

He nodded. "Spot on. Just a walk-through really. To make sure the lights were right. Barely necessary. These guys know exactly what they're doing and could give me what I want tonight without a problem. It was for my benefit really. I'll be more comfortable tonight knowing everything is working."

"You're a perfectionist," Daniel commented.

"To the point of distraction," Elijah laughed.

A cheery young waiter came to their table. "Something to drink, gentlemen? Something to eat?"

"Are you hungry?" Elijah asked, fixing him with his soulful brown eyes.

Suddenly Daniel found it hard to concentrate on anything else. "Err, actually I am," he said, realizing that he'd had nothing all day apart from coffee and orange juice at the hotel.

"How about sharing a pizza?" Elijah grinned. "Sound good?"

"Sounds perfect."

They ordered ham and mushroom and a beer each.

Being with Elijah was very natural. There was no uneasiness or awkwardness. Quite amazing when Daniel considered how much he fancied him.

"How did you go from having your own TV show to guesting on a cruise ship?" Daniel asked, then immediately regretted it. "Sorry. That came out blunter than I intended it to."

Elijah chuckled. "It is difficult to offend me."

"Weren't you in a sitcom after *Shades of England*? I don't remember much about it."

"Thank God for that," Elijah said. "It was called—"

"*Chips With That*," Daniel exclaimed. "Now I remember."

"Please don't," Elijah groaned. "A sitcom set in a greasy café. What can I say? I was desperate. I needed the money. I didn't write it. Thankfully the sorry mess was put out of its misery after only one season. Ultimately that awful show is the reason I'm here. TV work was a lot harder to find after two bona fide flops. I was bottom of the bill on *Saturday Night at the Apollo* and a last-minute replacement on *Would I Lie to You?* I got a couple of weeks doing warm up for *The Graham Norton Show*—off screen, you'll notice."

The waiter came back with their beers.

"Cheers," they said, clinking bottles.

"I'm struggling to accept that you couldn't get any TV work," Daniel said. Talking to him now, Elijah was as warm and charismatic as he was handsome. If only a fraction of that came across on TV, he would still be a winner.

"I got *some* work," he elaborated. "Before going into comedy, I trained at drama school to be an actor. So, I thought why not? Give it another shot. I soon remembered why I gave up acting in the first place. This." He drew a circle in the air around his face. "I'm half Greek and look like I come from the Middle East. For some casting directors that means just one thing—terrorist."

"No way," Daniel gasped.

"Oh yeah. If they wanted a swarthy-skinned man to play the villain, I was the go-to guy for a while. That's why I'm doing the cruise ships, because they allow me to play funny rather than evil."

Elijah spoke with good humor but there was something extremely shocking about what he had said. That producers and directors would be ignorant of his talent because of the shade of his skin.

The pizza arrived. It was huge with lashings of sauce and cheese.

"How about another beer?" Daniel suggested.

"Just the one then," Elijah said. "I've got a show to do, remember?"

They both grabbed a slice and ate. Daniel was pleased to see his enthusiasm for it. He wasn't one of those guys who worried about every carb or gram of fat. He'd dated men like that before and they were no fun.

"My turn to ask a question," Elijah said. "You won that talent show. You had a number-one record, if I remember correctly. I think my mum might even own one of your albums. What are *you* doing on the cruise ship circuit?"

Daniel swallowed and took a sip of beer. "It's a long story, but I'll give you the condensed version. Before I even entered that show, many years before, I used to work at sea. I was a singer in a ship's entertainment crew and loved it. I did numerous contracts and saw the world. I loved singing and traveling, so it was my dream job. I was in the middle of a contract when my dad took seriously ill. So that was it. I quit the ships and went home."

Elijah looked at him softly but didn't speak.

"I don't regret it," he maintained. "I got to be with my dad for his last few months and that was more important than anything else. But I never came back to sea and it's always felt like unfinished business. Before he died, my dad encouraged me to audition for *The One*. We used to watch it together when he was ill and he wanted me to do it. It made me the most clichéd of the talent show clichés, the boy singing for his dead dad, so I kept my backstory quiet. Anyway, after winning the show, my life took a crazy turn and I never looked back."

"So this is your unfinished business?" Elijah asked.

He nodded. "I promised myself at the start of this year that I would spend a few weeks at sea. My manager thinks I'm mad, but he's prepared to humor me on the condition I accept all the jobs he lines up on my return."

"I imagine he's pissed. Didn't you do some West End gigs? Big musicals. This must be quite a come down."

"Not at all. There'll be other gigs. This is only one summer."

Elijah's brow creased. "Has it been everything you were searching for?"

Daniel shrugged. "I wasn't searching for anything in particular. Just a sense of closure. Of completion. That's enough."

Which was the truth, he realized, until they had sat down for this lunch. He wasn't complete because he was alone. He didn't even know that before. He needed a man. A relationship. *Hell, a good fuck would do for a start.*

Sitting next to him was a man who could give him all those things.

Maybe. If he feels the same.

The ship would dock in Southampton on Sunday.

They had three days ahead of them to find out.

Chapter Four

Oliver Gill had spent the best part of the afternoon holed up in a hotel room with a couple of Dutch tourists and the holy trinity of mephedrone, crystal meth and GHB. Ordinarily, he wouldn't have gotten so wasted during the day, but it had been a good five weeks since he'd last indulged in a chemsex session. He had needed it. He had deserved it.

Since joining the company of the *Atlantic Anthem*, he had lived the life of a monk. A sober, frustrated and horny monk. So boring. He needed to let go a little.

When the ship had docked that morning, he'd known he had to get off and discover what Lisbon had to offer. They'd be going ape-shit in his absence, but his friend Shanitta would cover for him. He'd saved her arse enough times — she owed him.

Oliver should have been with the rest of the entertainment crew running through *Groovy Time*. But they could fuck off. He didn't need to rehearse. He could do that crap in his sleep. He was too good for them and deserved his own show, not some cheesy revue. No, with three nights on the ship remaining, he'd needed to have some fun.

He'd needed some cock.

When he'd logged onto Grindr and found the Dutch couple located just ten minutes' walk from the port, saying they were "horny and high", his mind was made up.

His balls had been turning blue, it had been so long. He'd had to get off. Fast.

The bedroom door had been ajar when he'd arrived. It looked and smelled like the two men, Paul and Rutger, had been at it for some time. Days in fact, judging from the stink.

The place was a mess. Clothes and empty bottles were strewn everywhere. It stank of sweat and smoke, alcohol, spunk and farts. The sheets were rumpled and dirty. A naked man had passed out on top. He lay on his front with his hips raised on pillows, his greasy arse open and accessible.

"That's Rutger," the second man, Paul, said. "He's a little out of it but don't let that stop you. You want his cunt, you take it. It's yours. It's everybody's."

Oliver closed and locked the door behind him.

Abusing the unconscious man was a tantalizing prospect but Oliver had more pressing urges. "Maybe later. Let's get high first."

Paul smiled, tugging his semi-hard dick and pointing toward the candy store laid on top of the dresser. After a couple of lines of mephedrone, Oliver sucked Paul's cock to state of full stiffness. It was sticky and tasted of lube. He could guess exactly where it had been before his mouth. The nasty thought drove him to suck even harder. Oliver was in a *very* slutty mood.

He'd be the dirtiest bitch in town if that was what they wanted.

After a couple of tokes of crystal, he undressed and let Paul fuck him on the floor doggy style. Big and hard, and raging with the drugs in his system, Paul gave it to him with some ferocious force. He even pulled out a couple of times and made him suck his dick before plunging it back into his hole. *Fuck, yeah.* These were the kind of wild, crazy times he missed when he was at sea.

Time became meaningless as their bodies and minds melted in a chemical-induced haze.

Rutger woke up and took a hit of GHB, of which Oliver and Paul also partook. Then it became really insane, fucking for all they were worth. In and out of each other's bodies.

Yes, this is it. Raunchy, raw sex. Fuck, yeah.

All those losers on board the *Anthem*. They spent

thousands on their cruise, thinking that stuffing their faces and pouring wine down their throats was the best way to enjoy themselves. *How sad. Pathetic.* They didn't know the first thing about pleasure. Most of them wouldn't know where to begin. Cock and chemicals and cum. They were ignorant of the real pleasures of the world. No need for a huge ship to enjoy them, just a big, hard dick.

Exhausted and spent, the he lay with the two men in a stupefied, stinking heap afterward. Rutger passed out again. *Messy cumdump.* Oliver would *never* let himself get in that state. It had been a while, at least.

He studied at them as they dozed. Damn, they weren't even that good-looking. Paul was around fifty and fat. *Ugh, gross.* He must have been outrageously horny when he'd stepped off the boat that morning to think *this* was acceptable. Still, he'd been with worse in the past and the drugs had helped. A lot.

He wondered if these guys were on PrEP. Probably should have inquired before he let them come inside him. Too late now. He'd go to the clinic when he got home. If he had time. If he remembered.

What time was it now? After four o'clock. *Sheeeeeet!* He'd been with these skanky old sluts for over five hours. Time to make a move. The ship sailed at six but everyone had to be back on board by five-thirty.

He got up to hunt for his clothes. His actions were kind of slow and woozy. He stumbled, landing flat on the floor, but found his shoes in the process. Giggling, he scrambled into his clothes as he came across them.

He knew he should get back to the ship. *What for? Something.* Something he had to do. *What was it? Oh yeah, Groovy Time.* He giggled again. *Groovy fucking Time.* The shitty seventies show. Could he sober up in time for that? No way. He was wasted.

Fully dressed, he headed for the door. "Bye, guys."

Paul and Rutger were both unconscious.

Oliver hesitated. It would be a shame not to take

advantage. Creeping back to the dresser, he examined what was left. There were a couple of small rocks of crystal. He'd be an ass to risk taking that on board. Besides, he'd never find a quiet place to smoke it undetected. There were two small bottles of GHB. One was three quarters empty and the other was completely full. *Perfect.*

He palmed the full bottle and left the room, not pausing until he reached the lobby. He ducked into the men's room and concealed the bottle in his underpants, tucking it safely behind his balls. His judgment might be addled with the drugs but he was as sharp as fox when it came to opportunity. *Look out for number one, motherfuckers.*

Time to get out of the hotel. Highly unlikely the fucked up Dutch men would come around anytime soon. They were so out of their heads, that they probably wouldn't wake up until tomorrow. By which time he'd be sailing north through the Bay of Biscay. *Ha. Stupid bastards.*

The late-afternoon sun blazed bright in a cloudless sky. Oliver cursed. He'd left his sunglasses on the ship. Shielding his eyes with his hands, he set off toward the port. The high effect of the drug cocktail was wearing off and he suddenly he was tired. How the hell would he pick himself up for that show tonight? He should have taken another hit of mephedrone or crystal before leaving the room. Neither of those bums would have noticed.

Jesus, it was hot. For late October, there was a lot of heat in the afternoon sun. He wiped his brow on the back of his arm, sweating profusely. Damn that GHB. He must have taken too much. It had already been mixed with vodka when Paul had given it to him. He had no idea of the dosage. *Those druggie bastards, it must have been way over the top.*

He needed an upper and fast if he would stand any chance of getting on stage tonight.

Fortunately it wasn't hard to score in Lisbon. A rancid old dealer with arthritic hands and stringy gray hair sold him a fifty-euro wrap of coke. It was most likely shit but he didn't have time to shop around. As long as its lifting effect got him through the evening, he'd be fine. Oliver stuffed the wrap into his underpants and hurried toward the port. It had gone five and they'd be sailing within the hour.

He raced up the gangplank with the remaining straggle of passengers. Once on board, he joined the line for security. He had no luggage so simply had to pass through the body scanner. He wasn't concerned. So long as the alarm didn't go off for a knife or a gun, those dopey fuckers let anyone through.

Eventually one of the guards, a formidable black man, nodded for him to step through the scanner. No alarm sounded, though the guard looked at him suspiciously.

"Is everything all right?"

Oliver froze and suffered a massive attack of paranoia. *He knows!* "Yes. Fine."

"You don't look too good." He pointed at Oliver's brow.

He lifted his hand. It was dripping with sweat. "Oh, yes. I…erm, lost track of the time and had to run back. It's hot out there."

The guy didn't appear convinced. *He doesn't believe me.* He looked intently at Oliver's eyes.

"You don't look well at all."

"I'm fine." His voice sounded high and strained. Which was exactly how he felt. He hastened for the entrance to the main crew area, expecting to feel a firm, detaining hand on his shoulder. When it didn't come, he bolted down the corridor to his cabin.

Thank God his roommate wasn't there. The beast from the house band he'd been forced to share with. The last thing Oliver wanted was to face the ugly bastard. He went straight to the mirror. *Fuck me! What a mess.* No wonder the security troll had looked at him strangely. It was a miracle they'd allowed him back on board.

His pupils were so wide they almost obscured his irises. His skin was waxy white and wet, while his bleached hair stuck up at crazy angles. Anyone with half a brain would look at him and know the truth, that he was off his face and royally fucked.

Getting worse, too. The come-down had most definitely started. With the daddy of all headaches, he hurt all over, more so in the butt, and just wanted to go to sleep. Sleep all the way to England. That would be nice.

No chance of that. If he missed the show Helen McDonald would make sure that he never worked on another cruise ship. She was like that. Cunty.

Though he was loath to admit it, even to himself, Oliver needed this job. Work in the UK had not been as plentiful as he liked to make out and he had used up most of his contacts there. Helen was a dreary, insipid old bitch, but he couldn't afford to burn that bridge just yet. He had to keep the cruise director on his side.

Stripping off his sour-smelling clothes, he stashed his drug haul in his underwear drawer and hit the shower. Fighting the lethargy the GHB had brought about, he washed himself thoroughly from head to toe, eliminating all surviving traces of the Dutch duo, then turned the water to cold, standing beneath the icy faucet for a full minute.

Shivering but somewhat revived, he dried himself and stood naked in front of the mirror. His body was thin and heavily tattooed. He ran his hands across his torso and proudly caressed his concave stomach and the plainly defined spaces between his ribs. He explored his midriff, minutely searching for surplus of flesh. There was none. He was in fine condition. Satisfied, Oliver dressed quickly in clean jeans and a shirt.

He extracted the wrap of cocaine from his drawer. Okay, he'd have to eke this out across the night to keep himself going. A little now, a bit more around eight o'clock then a big hit right before the show. By one in the morning, he could fall into bed exhausted.

He'd be fine by tomorrow and would have most of the day to himself. He could sleep late. Maybe make a play for that dishy comedian. Elijah someone or other. He was a horny-looking bastard. They could partake of a little of his

GHB and fuck their brains out. *That* sounded like a very good plan.

Oliver cut himself a modest line of coke and snorted. The satisfying cold sensation hit his nostrils straight away. Hmm, this stuff wasn't as shitty as he'd expected. That crusty old dealer had done good.

Someone knocked on the cabin door.

"Just a sec." He put the wrap in his pocket and rubbed the residue from the dresser around his gums. *Damn, this stuff is good.*

"It's me, Shanitta. Open up."

Shanitta's eyes widened at the sight of him. Oliver pulled out a pair of clean socks and continued getting dressed.

Shanitta D'Costa, with her tightly pinched face, was essentially the mirror imagine of Oliver. She stomped into the room in a gray leotard and black hoodie. "You're wired," she remarked, leaning against the dresser and looking him up and down.

"I'm fine," he said. The coke had already taken effect. He was brighter already. If he could just maintain the slight high all night, he'd be all right. "Am I in trouble?"

"Big trouble, I'd say. Like, major. They are not 'appy at all that you missed rehearsal. I told 'em you was sick, man, but Orestis called the gangway. He knows you disembarked, so you'd better 'ave a good story ready. He's given your solo to Vladislav tonight."

"*The Russian?* Why? He's a shit singer."

"Yeah, but he was at rehearsal and you wasn't. Orestis made us rework the show without you. I don't think he'll let you go on tonight."

"We'll see about that," Oliver said, full of cocaine confidence. "I'll talk the old fart 'round. No tone-deaf Russian is going to steal my song."

"You won't have 'eard about Vlad then," Shanitta said cheerily.

"Oh, God, what now?"

"He spent the night with that comedian."

"Elijah," Oliver screamed.

"That's 'im. Vlad is keeping schtum about it but everyone is talking about them."

"That cock-sucking Russian slut," Oliver fumed. "I wanted Elijah. He was on my to-do list for this weekend. Now I'll have to make do with Vlad's sloppy seconds."

"Sloppy seconds? I thought that was you, babes." Shanitta chuckled.

"Sloppy, never. I've got the tightest ring on this ship. Something Elijah will find out for himself soon enough."

They both laughed.

* * * *

Helen McDonald sat behind her desk with a stern face. Orestis Mendes stood behind her with his arms folded and did all the talking. *A lot of fucking talking.*

Oliver had been stuck in the chair before them, listening to it for fifteen minutes. No, not really listening. He tuned in and out, nodding when he thought it appropriate and making suitably contrite noises. Let them have their say and get it off their chests. It would make them feel better, like they were in charge.

But all three of them knew the truth. He was the best singer and dancer in their company. The passengers *loved* him. He'd been on TV. None of the other fuckers had. Helen and Orestis couldn't afford to let him go. There's be a mutiny.

Orestis was the director of all the house shows. A sallow-skinned, balding little man. He'd smoked too many cigarettes and sucked too many cocks. It had given his face an unfortunate pinched look. *Haggard, like the old queen he was.*

"For the last time, where were you today?" Orestis asked. *"Really."*

"I already told you," Oliver said meekly. "I didn't feel too good so I went ashore to sort myself out. I just needed to feel some steady ground beneath my feet, that's all."

"You seemed fine when I saw you this morning," Helen said. "You didn't say anything about being ill."

"It came on suddenly."

"But you didn't see the ship's medic?" Orestis needled.

"Just a touch of sea sickness, that's all. Feet on terra firma and a couple of aspirin, it soon sorted me out. There was nothing to trouble the doctor with."

"You were AWOL," Orestis said firmly. "You didn't inform anyone that you were sick."

"I told Shanitta."

"Shanitta is not responsible for you. I am."

"I'm sorry. It won't happen again. I wasn't thinking straight. It'll never happen again."

Helen and Orestis exchanged a meaningful look. The fuckers had it in for him. *Well, screw them. I'm Oliver Gill. Famous, for God's sake.* No one had heard of this pair outside this crusty ship. They thought they were something special but they were nothing. Nobodies. He'd been on the telly. These twats hadn't.

He could do with another toot of coke. That first line was wearing off already.

"Are you up to performing tonight?" Helen asked.

"Absolutely. I feel much better now. One thousand percent."

"You look washed out."

"No, I'm good. I can do the show."

"All right," Orestis said. "I'll let you perform, but Vladislav will sing *Night Fever*."

"Hey, that's my song. He'll never manage the falsetto with his dreary voice."

"He managed fine in run-through. You're on backup. Vladislav takes the lead. He's rehearsed and he sounds good. Very good."

Motherfucker!

"Okay," he said reluctantly. He'd get them back for this. He didn't know how, not yet, but he would. This was a total diss. "Is that all?"

"Consider yourself fortunate," Helen said. "Competition for your job is tough. If you're not cut out for this there are plenty of talented people who are."

"Yes, Helen. I appreciate it." *Like hemorrhoids, you old hag.* "Thank you."

He stood to leave. As he rose, he caught sight of an image on Helen's computer screen. A man. He had dark hair—a good-looking face. Oliver froze. It looked like… No. It couldn't be.

"Who is that?" he asked, angling for a better look. It was a black-and-white professional portrait. The face of the man was strong. And handsome. *Too fucking handsome.*

"That's Daniel Blake. He's tomorrow night's headliner. I'm just putting together the info for the guests," Helen said.

He was still numb from the effect of the drugs and the name pierced his addled brain, having an immediately sobering effect.

Daniel Blake.

Daniel. Fucking. Blake.

Not him. Not again.

Shit. Fuck. Goddamn it.

Would he ever hear the last of that bastard?

Chapter Five

With a cold beer in hand, Daniel stood on the top deck of the *Anthem* and took in the spectacle of the great ship setting sail. The sky was darkening with splendid flashes of orange and red across a palate of deepening blue. A lot of passengers had taken advantage of the warm evening to come up top and enjoy the final sail-away of their holiday.

Glasses of champagne, prosecco and colorful cocktails were being drunk all around him. People were heading home and determined to make the most of the remaining time. Every moment mattered. Music blasted across the deck, heady Latin rhythms that kept everybody in the carnival mood.

Daniel was excited about going home too. He was looking forward to seeing his family, catching up with friends, spending time in his own house and sleeping in his own bed. All the comforts of home he took for granted until he was away. He worked all over the world but was a 'home' boy at heart.

The ship passed beneath the Twenty-Fifth of April Bridge, a stunning creation based on the design of San Francisco's Golden Gate Bridge, as it made its way to the ocean. As the vessel slid under the structure with barely a meter to spare, applause rippled around the deck.

Daniel gazed upward in awe. It was moments like this that made traveling worthwhile.

He was in a brilliant mood and had the whole evening ahead of him.

He'd been invited to dine at the captain's table. That was a first.

As he'd explored the ship that afternoon, he'd encountered the man himself in the crew hallway with Helen. Usually so calm and professional, Helen had gone to pieces in front of him, like a girl with a crush on her favorite teacher.

He couldn't blame the poor woman. Captain Roman Rassimov was as dashing as his name implied. Tall and brooding, he had thick black hair and chiseled features. In his sharp white uniform, he was a dream come true.

"Welcome back," he had said, pumping Daniel's hand. His forearms were muscular and hairy. He spoke with a deep Italian accent. "I'm sorry I didn't meet you properly last time you were here."

"It's an honor you remember me at all," Daniel replied, looking into his eyes. They were as deep as the Atlantic itself. "On the maiden voyage, you had a lot going on."

"I caught some of your act on the opening night. I see a lot of performers at sea, Daniel, but I only remember the very best."

Helen beamed. "When Captain Rassimov told us how much he enjoyed your show, I just had to have you back."

"The first of many visits, I hope," the captain said.

He was a charmer all right. No wonder Helen was smitten, working so closely with him.

"Join me at my table tonight," he said. "I dine at eight-thirty."

"It would be an honor."

Eight-thirty was perfect and suited his plans just fine. As exciting as it was to be invited to the handsome captain's table, there was someone on board who'd had a bigger impact on him. Elijah Mann.

Wow.

Daniel still didn't know what had happened when they'd met but it was something quite seismic. He had never felt such an immediate attraction to anyone. It was the kind of thing he sang about in songs, emotions he had only experienced through lyrics until now. But this afternoon it had happened for real.

Elijah's first show was scheduled for seven-thirty. Daniel planned to get ready early and catch the set before joining the captain for dinner. He was excited. He hadn't been joking when he'd told Elijah he was a fan of his TV show. It was genius. He loved it and couldn't wait to see him live. In person, he was so much sexier than what came across on screen.

And had he imagined it or was Elijah interested in him too? The way he'd looked at him throughout lunch and held his eye. There was something there. *Wishful thinking?* It could be. *What did it matter?*

They had nowhere else to go until Sunday. He would check out his show and hopefully, if he was lucky, get to know him afterward. What happened next, they would have to wait and see.

With twenty minutes to spare before he'd have to change, Daniel took a stroll around the deck, reacquainting himself with the upper levels of the *Anthem*. As they cleared the port and headed out to sea, a fresh breeze blew across the deck and the ship pitched on the waves. The stability of big, modern ships like this was so advanced that it could be deceptive, giving the sensation of not moving at all.

But he loved the motion. They were on the ocean and he wanted to feel it. If he wanted stillness, he would stay home.

A cool sea breeze rippled through his hair. That was a special feeling.

In the forward section of the deck, he found the leisure and beauty facilities — hairdressers, spa and gym. Not his thing. He hated being fussed over. Whenever he appeared on TV he found the whole hair and makeup aspect the worst part of the experience. Strangers invading his space and getting too personal with their brushes and scissors.

He didn't understand why people submitted themselves to that for pleasure. *No, thank you.*

The gym was different. He didn't enjoy it but accepted it was a necessary evil. Looking good and maintaining a decent level of fitness were essential to his work. He had to be in pristine shape every time he went on stage.

The gym was well-equipped. As good as any he'd used on shore. Like everything on this ship, it was designed to the highest standard. There were twenty cross trainers, twenty treadmills, vibro-plates, cycles, rowing machines, free weights and resistance trainers.

There were plenty of machines in use. Even at this time of night the gym was two-thirds full. Daniel had neither the time nor the motivation to train tonight. But tomorrow — show day — he would be here. A good total-body workout before breakfast would set him up for the day.

From Deck Sixteen it was easier to take the stairs to his stateroom on Ten than to wait for the elevator. There was plenty to enjoy on the wide staircases. Original artwork hung on the walls with large statement pieces situated at each turn in the stairs. Predominantly modern art, much of its meaning went over his head, but he appreciated it the same.

Daniel had descended to as far as Fourteen when a voice called out from above.

"Just a minute, Mr. Blake. Hold on."

There was an accent, perhaps New Zealand, but he didn't recognize the voice. Someone after a selfie? He didn't want to be rude but time was running out. He was pushing it to catch Elijah's show already.

A pair of pale white legs appeared on the stairs — they were like match sticks — rising to a pair of jade-green running shorts. Their owner came into view. A tall, thin man with white hair. The rest of his body was as long and scrawny as his legs, all the way to the top of his head. Not just skinny — he was emaciated.

He smiled, displaying oversized, perfectly straight white teeth.

Yikes, thought Daniel, *those teeth can't be nature's own.*

He looked like a grinning horse.

"Hi," he said, coming forward. His voice was nasal in tone. "Don't look so worried. I can see what you're thinking

51

but I'm *not* one of your fans."

Daniel smiled weakly.

Who the hell is this?

"I wanted to introduce myself," the man said, grinning, dissecting Daniel with cold eyes, head to toe and back again. "I'm Terry St. King. Resident entertainer. No doubt you've heard of me."

Oh, boy. The *Terry St. King.* The *Anthem's* resident piano man. His diva reputation was legendary.

"Of course, Terry. Wow. It's a pleasure to meet you. I've heard so much about you. All over Europe in fact. It doesn't matter what ship I'm on, I've heard your name mentioned." He was laying it on thick, but better to keep the old boy sweet. He would only bitch otherwise.

Terry tried and failed to look self-depreciative. "It's true. I do have quite a following. People tell me all the time how they book their cruises based specifically on my schedule. Isn't that something?"

Something? It was insane but Daniel nodded, stoking his ego. "I can believe it. People speak so highly of you. You're lucky to have such a loyal following."

'*A dinosaur. A fossil. A has-been who was never anything to begin with.*' Those were some of the kinder comments he'd heard about the piano man this season. Years ago, when he'd first worked the ships, before he'd auditioned for *The One*, Terry's reputation had been legendary. Their paths had never crossed, but he'd always had a morbid curiosity about the singer who'd generated such a reputation. In person, he was much as he'd imagined, only thinner and older.

Terry came down the steps and took Daniel's elbow in a pincer-sharp grip. "I know you're very busy, Dan. C'mon, I won't keep you. Let's walk and talk. It'll be fun."

Up close it was obvious that Terry was wearing makeup. *To the gym.* The white power had gone greasy with sweat and clumps had formed in the creases around his eyes and mouth. His hair was white and very frou frou. It looked as natural as his teeth.

"I *do* hope you are not too busy to come and see me play."

"I'd be delighted."

"You'll find me in the Moonlight Lounge. I'm there most nights. It's an *intimate* venue but I do like it. Helen, bless her, thinks my act is suited to such surroundings, and it is of course, but not everyone can get to see me there. Earlier in the season I was doing a headline shows in the theater most weeks. Two shows a night until Helen decided I was more suited to matinee performances. Now she doesn't even want me for that. I'm *wasted* here."

"I'm sure that's not true. You must pack that lounge each night."

"It's *not* the same. Oh, you wouldn't know about that, Dan. Not yet. You're still reasonably young and the flavor of the moment. It's always easier when you've done telly too. We didn't rely on what they call TV *talent* shows to make a name when I started. We had to rely on simple talent and garnering a reputation. You're the headliner. You should enjoy that. For now. While you can."

Terry's eyes burned into the side of his head. They reached Deck Ten. *Thank God.*

"I'll bear that in mind," Daniel said. "This is my floor. I don't want to be rude but I really need to change in a hurry."

Terry didn't relax the grip on his elbow. "*Ten*. You're on Deck Ten?" The oily smarm vanished from his voice. Now it was pure steel.

"Yes. Like I said, this is my floor."

Terry's eyes narrowed to tiny slits. "This is a passenger deck. Why aren't you staying below with the rest of the crew?"

Daniel put his hand on top of Terry's and pulled it off his arm. "I don't know. I didn't ask for it. I came on board this afternoon and went where I was told to. This was my allocation."

"Huh," the piano man sneered. "Sixty years in show business count for nothing on this floating heap. No offense,

53

Dan, but it's come to something when veteran performers get passed over for two bit upstarts with five minutes of TV fame. The matinee show you're doing on Saturday afternoon, that was *my* slot until this week."

Daniel took a deep breath. He'd had more than enough of this faded diva and his barely veiled insults. "Look, for a start, my name is Daniel, not Dan. I'm not a Dan. Second, I'm sorry you feel you've been pushed out of the theater but it had nothing to do with me. I was hired to perform three shows and that's what I'm here to do. When and where those shows go on doesn't matter. The main theater or the pool bar, I don't care, I'll do my show wherever they want it. Helen is the cruise director and makes the decisions. If you've got a problem with your booking then you need to take it up with her, not me."

Terry's oily smile snapped back into place. "I think you misunderstand me—"

"No," Daniel said firmly. "I understand you very well. You're pissed off and I understand why that might be. But it's not my problem. There are enough waves at sea, Terry, I'm not here to make more. You need to address your issues with Helen—she's the one who can do something about it."

Terry's face hardened. Looking at Daniel with fresh, predatory eyes, he said, "You're very sure of yourself, aren't you?"

"I'm paid to do a good job. That's why I'm here, just like you. I'll certainly come to see your show but for now, excuse me, I'm running very late."

Before Terry could utter another word, he turned and strode along the corridor to his room. Rivalry and bitchiness were the worst parts of show business. He'd experienced it at every level. Stoking the fires of jealousy got you nowhere. He'd met men and women like Terry before. No one could reason with their bitterness, just leave them to it.

He had more important matters. Elijah's show. He would not miss that for the sake of some toxic old queen.

* * * *

Insolent upstart. What a bastard.

Terry St. King seethed as the younger man walked away. He had turned his back on him as if he was nobody. Like he was one of the daggy passengers. The ego of the man. Five minutes on some crappy TV show and he acted like the king of the sea.

Has Daniel Blake sung Rodgers and Hart for Princess Diana? No, he fucking hasn't. Shared a bill with Shirley Bassey and Bonnie Tyler? Played Las Vegas, New York and Hollywood? No way. Because he is nobody.

Terry stomped down the stairs. He had a show of his own at eight-thirty and needed to get some of the anger out of his system.

Passengers, delighted to see him, passed him on the descent.

"Hi, Terry." A colossal American bitch beamed. "I do hope you'll sing *Misty* tonight."

"Hello, dear." His smile was as artificial as the teeth within it. "Can't stop. Busy, busy, busy."

The passengers adored him — as rightly they should.

They recognized show biz royalty when they saw it. Some of them did anyway. The other half were content with the commercial crap Helen spoon fed them on the main stage. *Bloody jugglers and acrobats. She has a frigging comedian in there tonight. The stupid bitch has lost her mind. Too busy chasing the captain's cock to see what a disaster she's made of the entertainment lineup.*

Daniel Blake played the game well enough. He had his tongue so far up Helen's arse he could lick her tonsils. That was obviously what everyone had to do to make it on this ship. But Terry couldn't lower himself to that. Not a chance. The woman was a moron. He would never be nice to her. Even if it meant headline theater shows and a stateroom on Deck Ten.

Those things should be his by right, not because he sucked

up to Helen.

But Daniel knew what he was doing. That sort always did. Ruthless bastard.

He is dolly enough. Terry would give him that. And Helen was a sucker for a pretty face. *The old whore. He's young enough to be her son, but if she thinks there's a chance of a poke she'll take it. That would explain the stateroom. So she won't get caught dropping her knickers in crew quarters.*

What a tawdry ship this was. Despite the trappings of luxury, it was nothing more than a glorified knocking shop at sea.

Terry reached the sanctuary of his cabin on Deck Two. There were no windows, not even a porthole, but at least he didn't have to share with one of the other plebs. That was something. If Helen had her way, he'd be sleeping on a bunk in the engine room.

Somehow, Terry had made the room his own, investing it with a modicum of sparkle and glamour. A fur throw on the single bed, bejeweled picture frames, photos of himself with world famous celebrities—Shirley Bassey, Joan Collins, Cilla Black, Sheena Easton, Olivia Newton-John and his beloved Princess Diana. Pride of place on the wall was a framed newspaper review of the performance he had given for Diana. Precious memories that kept him sane.

This was his special place. Away from all the riff raff. A place to compose himself before facing the crowd.

Terry poured a three-inch shot of gin with the tiniest dribble of tonic and sank into the armchair he'd filched from a public lounge.

He raised his glass to the picture of Diana.

"You're in a better place than I am, my dear. Cheers."

He drained the gin in a single draught.

Chapter Six

"There aren't many people in," Elijah remarked

"You're not due on for another fifteen minutes. There's plenty of time. Relax," Anouska said.

They stood in the shadows at the side of the stage, gazing into the auditorium.

"They're filling up the seats at the back. The entire front section is empty."

"They always do that. Come on, you know the game by now. You've played enough ships to know how it works."

Indeed he had, but he was nervous tonight — totally out of character. He wanted a full house. The odds were against him for the early show. The ship was late leaving port tonight amid a splendid sunset. People had made the most of it and lingered on deck for longer. There was no great rush for the theater, not with everything else that was going on. They could have an extra drink in the starlight or enjoy a cocktail in one of the bars or saloons. Some folk would loiter in their staterooms, making love, taking time to get ready. There was no rush — it was only a comic on stage tonight.

Every cruise was the same, having to compete with so many other activities. It didn't really matter. He was paid the same whether the house was full or half empty. It wasn't as if he got a percentage of the door.

He couldn't take it personally.

But he did.

And tonight was no different. He wanted a decent house. Why? Daniel of course. It was easy to get a reaction from a full house. He didn't want Daniel coming by to find him getting half-hearted laughs from a lackluster crowd. He wanted Daniel to see him in top form, with an audience in stitches.

Slim chance of that.

The people who bothered to get in early spread themselves out at the back of the theater. A dozen or so were dotted among the first three rows and there was a vast space in between. The entire mid-section was bare. He knew the game. They sat at the back so that if he was shit, they could make a hasty exit.

"I'll die on my arse out there," he grumbled.

"Give it a rest," Anouska said. "Come on. Back to your dressing room. Relax for ten minutes. Drink your whiskey. I might have a wee dram with you."

It was a tradition he had taken up years ago, and over time it had turned into a superstition. He had a double measure of good scotch before going on stage. It settled his nerves and brought him luck. It helped with the voice too.

They went to the guest dressing room and shut the door. Elijah poured two slugs of scotch while Anouska lined up some tunes on his iPod. An old Donna Summer album began to play.

"Disco?" he remarked.

"You're not the only one who has a show tonight. I have to get in the zone."

"Is that why you've done up your hair like that?"

"Funny," she said dryly, accepting her glass.

Anouska was partially made up in her *Groovy Time* outfit. Though she wore a white dressing gown and slippers, her usually red hair was stowed beneath a huge Farrah Fawcett wig. Her makeup was heavily applied with lashings of blue and purple and she wore three pairs of false eyelashes. She took her first sip of whiskey, leaving a glittering lipstick smear on the glass.

Elijah swallowed deeply, enjoying the mellow warmth as it flowed down his throat.

"You've had quite an effect on Vladislav," Anouska said.

"Oh, don't remind me. Why? What's he said?"

"Nothing. He wouldn't blab. But he's been in a good mood all afternoon. *Smiling*. And he never smiles. Not when he's off stage, anyway. I'd say you've put quite the spring in the boy's step."

"I wish I hadn't. I wish I had done nothing with him at all."

I wish I'd saved myself for Daniel.

"What's the big deal? It was just a shag. God, it can't have been all that bad. I know he's not exactly loaded with charisma but he's easy on the eye with a body to die for."

"You wouldn't understand."

"You're right. I don't. If you don't want to see him again, no one will force you, but don't act like it's some major incident. You're two grown men who had a fuck. End of."

Elijah smiled. Anouska had a knack for saying the right thing at exactly the right time. He needed a verbal bitch-slap and she gave it.

There was a knock on the door.

"Five-minute call," yelled the stage director.

Elijah downed the rest of his drink. *Time to go to work.* He wondered whether Daniel had taken a seat yet. It didn't matter. He had to stop thinking about him or how many people were in the crowd. It was time to focus and deliver an awesome show for the people who had turned up. That was his concern now.

He wanted to be the talk of the ship tonight. In the restaurants and bars afterward, he wanted them to say, *Oh, you should have seen him. The funniest show I've seen in ages. You really missed out.* He wanted everyone who didn't come in to regret the decision.

"I'd better make tracks," Anouska said, finishing her drink. "Have a marvelous show. Will I see you upstairs for a boogie later?"

"Probably. If I make it out of here alive. I'll be there."

"Groovy." She blew him a kiss and left.

Elijah checked his appearance in the mirror. It wasn't too

bad. He hated suits and ties but going on stage in anything less was frowned upon. T-shirts and jeans were fine for the comedy clubs back home but not posh ships. The full tux was preferred but he compromised with a slim-fitting blue suit, pale blue shirt and thin red tie. Very James Bond. It looked good under the stage lights too.

"Veeeeerry nice." The voice from behind startled him. Anouska had left the door open.

A thin-faced man stood in the frame, staring — no, leering — at Elijah's reflection. He was dressed like a member of a Bee Gees tribute band. Flared trousers, platform shoes, a tight shirt open to the navel and a tangle of medallions resting on a narrow, hairless chest. He wore a huge bouffant wig. Barry Gibb, circa nineteen-seventy-nine.

Obviously, a *Groovy Time* dancer.

"If you're looking for Anouska, you just missed her. She went to get ready. If you're quick, you should catch her."

The man leaned on one side of the frame, sticking his hips forward. The unnatural bulge in his trousers could only be padding. It was ridiculous. "Anouska? Why the hell would I want her? Elijah, it's you I was looking for." His lips puckered into a suggestive moue.

Elijah raised his eyebrows.

What is this? A joke? It had to be. Anouska trying to set him up after the Vladislav debacle.

"I'm about to go on stage." He smiled, keeping it friendly, holding back what he wanted to say — 'get lost, mate.'

The visitor in Bee Gees drag licked his lips. "I'm Oliver. I've got a show myself so I won't keep you. I just wanted to drop by and invite you to a party. A private *par-tay*. Know what I'm saying? Just the two of us. Later tonight. We can get to know each other. Get high. It could be a lot of fun."

Oh God, this isn't a joke. It was a genuine come-on. And Oliver was off his tits. Elijah had been around enough drugged messes to recognize when one was making a pass at him. The dead-eyed stare, the sweat on the top lip and brow, the agitated movements... Oliver was wired.

And on a ship. *What an utter dickhead.* He was lucky that the next stop was England. Anyone caught in possession of drugs would be put off at the next port, into police custody.

On stage, the band played *You Can't Stop the Beat* from *Hairspray*. It was the theme Helen used for her entrance every night. Which meant two minutes to show time. Helen would welcome the audience then introduce his act.

Oliver licked his lips lasciviously once more and thrust his hips farther forward.

"Listen," Elijah spoke slowly and clearly so the message would get through to Oliver's addled brain. "I don't *party* in that way. Ever. Know what I'm saying? Now, I'm due on stage."

Oliver did not try to move as he approached the door.

"How about a cheeky blow job after the show? I'm a fine cock sucker. Ask anyone. Once I get you off, you'll change your mind about everything else. All the men I've blown agree." He licked his lips for emphasis and lowered his voice to a husky growl. "They say I'm the best little cock sucker at sea."

"Mate, I'm honestly not interested. Now get out of my way." He roughly shoved Oliver aside and dashed into the wings.

Helen reached the end of her introduction. "Now, ladies and gentlemen, you're in for a real treat. So put your hands together and give this guy a huge *Anthem* welcome. Elijah Mann."

The crowd applauded. The band played. Elijah took a breath and stuck out his chest.

He was on.

* * * *

His fears were unwarranted.

He reached the end of the first act, closing the show with his funny song and dance routine, and the audience was on their feet. The applause was rapturous.

He wallowed in their response. It didn't get better than this. Though the theater was only half full, it was better than he'd expected.

He had to work hard in the first show. The audience wasn't quite on side, no doubt wondering if they'd made the right choice or whether they'd be better off elsewhere, but he won them over. Those initial laughs, civil and reserved, had become spontaneous and uncontrolled. By the end, they were on their feet again.

He returned to his dressing room in a happier state than when he'd left. He shut the door behind him to discourage any further booty calls. Whoever that Oliver person was, he could do without him.

There was an hour until his next show. Elijah knew exactly who he wanted to spend that time with. He flipped his tablet computer to life and entered Daniel's name into a search engine. That was one of the benefits of meeting someone famous, they could be Googled to discover more than a few drunken Facebook pictures.

He started with Daniel's bio page on Wikipedia, as good a place as any to crib a few facts. The photo at the top of the article was a few years old, taken soon after his successful win on *The One*. He looked kind of cute, younger and thinner faced with a slightly longer hairstyle. Still very good-looking, but not as drop-dead handsome as the man he'd met today.

Daniel had grown up in Leeds. That much was obvious from his accent. He had joined a boyband when he was sixteen. That was something Elijah hadn't known. They had been called Overload. He'd never heard of them. The article said they'd released three singles and an album.

Intrigued, Elijah navigated to YouTube and searched for the band. He quickly found a video for their first single. A cover version of the ELO hit *All Over the World*. He hit play and immediately began to laugh as the video rolled. It was totally of its time. A cheesy full-out pop tune that was faster and cheaper-sounding than the original.

As a band, Overload appeared to be a manufactured musical product. Five cute guys in sleeveless shirts, running through an energetic dance routine. Elijah stared open-mouthed at Daniel. He was so young. Much younger looking than any of the boys around him. He was little more than a child. Skinny and immature, his face was narrow, giving his teeth an oversized, horsey look.

Elijah felt guilty for watching. It was the pop-music equivalent of someone's mother bringing out the childhood photos to show a new boyfriend. But he couldn't stop. When the video finished, he clicked another, then another. *How come I've never heard of this band before?* They might only have had a handful of singles but there were plenty of clips to watch. Videos, *Top of the Pops*, Saturday morning TV shows. He realized he was three years older than Daniel. If Overload was going when Daniel was sixteen, at nineteen, he would have been far too old and cool to take notice of anything so poppy.

It was fun to hear it now. Enough time had passed that Overload was starting to look and sound retro.

Elijah was so caught up in the video loop that the five-minute call for act two took him by surprise.

The second show was much easier than the first. The crowd was on his side from the start. It helped that most of them had had a drink or three with dinner. They were in a better mood and more amenable to his jokes. Word must have spread after the first act and the theater was full.

He reveled in the applause for as long as he dared — it wouldn't do to outstay his welcome.

"Thank you, ladies and gentlemen, you've been great," he yelled. "Get off and enjoy the rest of your evening. Goodnight."

The applause remained electric as he left the stage. Helen McDonald was waiting in the wings.

"Well done, love. You smashed that." She tottered onto the stage to wrap up the show and direct the audience toward the remaining entertainment. "Elijah Mann, ladies and gentlemen. Didn't I tell you he was good?"

Another cheer followed.

Elijah grinned. He had indeed smashed it.

Leaving the stage was like entering a rapid decompression unit. From bright lights and adulation to the reality behind the façade. The technical crew, dressed in black, rushed to close it all down before either moving on to their next job or going to bed. There was rarely a quiet moment behind the scenes.

But for now, he was done.

Elijah headed straight back to the dressing room. There was a natural come-down when he left the stage — a depression. The trick to avoiding it was to keep moving. But first he had to get out of this damn suit. He burned serious energy going through the routine, combined with the heat of the lights, his clothes were always soaked with sweat when he came off.

He stripped immediately to the waist and used the balled-up shirt to wipe down his torso. The air conditioning was switched on and he felt better already. He poured himself a celebratory whisky.

Groovy Time was due to kick off in the Sky Lounge at eleven-forty-five. He had an hour. There was no way he could ever go to bed straight after a show. Going to his cabin would only accelerate the come-down. He'd rather be with other people. Anyway, he had promised Anouska he'd be there for her show.

That weird guy, Oliver, would also be there. *The best little cock sucker at sea.* What was he all about?

He hoped this had nothing to do with Vladislav. Anouska was adamant that the Russian was not a kiss-and-tell type, but gossip had clearly spread among the company. Did the resident crew now see him as some kind of easy lay? A piece of meat for the taking?

Even if he wanted to put it about, Oliver would be the last man on his list. Too skinny for a start. He liked men who were men, not trying to be little boys. Then there were the drugs. People could do what they wanted if it made them happy but he wouldn't be part of it. He'd seen the harm drugs did. At best, they made the users boring and annoying, at worst they consumed them.

And this whole business of getting off one's head to have sex was pathetic. If a person couldn't enjoy sex for what it was, they were doing it wrong. Very wrong.

Oliver seemed to think he was hot stuff. The opposite was true. He was a big turnoff.

There was another knock on the dressing room door.

Without thinking he called, "Yeah."

The door opened. *Oh, shit, this better not be Oliver again. I don't even have a shirt on.*

But the face he saw was one hundred percent preferable. Daniel Blake.

"Sorry," Daniel said. "I didn't know you were dressing."

Suddenly Elijah got very excited. *Be cool.* "It's okay. Come in. Nothing to see that you haven't got yourself." *Bad line – don't be a douche.* "I just have to do a quick change. It's so hot on that stage."

Daniel entered, closed the door and leaned against it. "I know what you mean. I'm not surprised either. You worked your butt off out there. Hell of a good show."

"You saw it?"

"Actually, I caught the early one. I wanted to drop by in the interval but had to rush to dinner."

Daniel wore a black tux. He'd loosened the tie and undone the top few buttons of his shirt. Some men could pull off a tuxedo. Others looked like gorillas in suits. Daniel was 007 debonair.

"You look smart," Elijah said, making no effort to dress, holding in his stomach, lifting his chest.

Daniel shrugged. "I had to borrow it. I had an invite to the captain's table."

"You lucky sod. I'll forgive you for passing me over in the interval. How was it?"

"Really nice. Good food, a great host, great company."

"The captain's quite a dish, eh?"

Daniel chuckled. "I'm sure Helen agrees."

Daniel's gaze followed him, drifting slowly over Elijah's torso. He ambled to the closet. If Daniel liked what he saw it would be rude to deny him. He had a fresh shirt hanging up, black with short sleeves. He took his time. He was showing off. Why not? He might not get another chance.

"Anyway," Daniel continued, "I came by to congratulate you. That was a brilliant show. I haven't laughed so much in ages. The audience loved you too."

Elijah slowly fastened his shirt. "I got them there eventually."

"I, er" — Daniel suddenly looked shy — "was wondering. If you're not sick of my company after lunch, if you wanted to check out this show in the Sky Lounge tonight. It's all disco music. We could have a drink. It might be fun."

Elijah realized he wasn't breathing. For a moment, everything seemed to have stopped.

"I'd love to. My friend is a dancer in that show so I'm heading that way too. I'd love the company."

He couldn't tell if Daniel was asking him out or just being friendly. It was a step in the right direction, but he realized he was more nervous now than when he'd done his show.

Chapter Seven

The show had already begun when they reached the Sky Lounge. Daniel didn't mind. They had taken their time getting there. Daniel was keen to check out Terry St. King's lounge act first.

"Really?" Elijah said, when he told him. "I hear he's terrible."

"I'm curious," Daniel explained. "He pulled a bit of a diva act on me earlier. I want to see if he's as good as he thinks he is."

He wasn't.

The Moonlight Lounge was one of the smaller venues on the ship, not much bigger than an ordinary living room, but it was packed. Daniel and Elijah squeezed through the door and stood against the back wall. The average age of the audience was around seventy.

Terry sat haughtily at his piano and talked his way through the songs with little attempt at singing. Even then his voice was a thin, nasally drawl.

Daniel hated being bitchy but he couldn't imagine how this act would ever play in a large theater.

"Heard enough?" Elijah asked, after a couple of songs.

"Oh, yeah."

Terry was awful, but spending time with Elijah was a real pleasure. He was droll and funny and gorgeous. Walking in on him shirtless was the highlight of an already memorable day. Those shoulders and that hairy chest. *Wow.* It was exactly the kind of body Daniel lusted after, manly and strong but not too perfect. Daniel was not a fan of the overly defined six-pack and was pleased to see that neither was Elijah.

It was early but there was already something going on between them. Physical attraction for sure, but there was something else. Chemistry? Heat? Whatever it was, he felt it all the way. As they rode in the lift, it came off them in waves. He couldn't keep his eyes off Elijah.

They came out of the elevator on Deck Fifteen. Music blasted from the Sky Lounge, a bombastic version of *Boogie Wonderland*. The deck beneath their feet throbbed with the tempo.

"Whoa, I think we just stepped back in time," Elijah said. "Forty years or so."

"It's Studio 54 at sea," Daniel agreed. "We're here now, might as well join the party."

The Sky Lounge, probably the most chic and sophisticated of the *Anthem's* bars, had been transformed into a nineteen-seventies discotheque. Glitter balls spun on the ceiling, casting their magical reflections around the room. The *Anthem* band was crowded on the stage while the dancers took over the floor. The entire group was dressed in seventies fashions. Halter-neck tops, flares, hot pants, leotards, fur coats, sequined jackets and a huge assortment of wigs, covering all popular hairstyles of the era.

A couple of the dancers stood at the front of the stage, performing live vocals with the band, while the others got the audience into the party spirit, teaching the dance moves.

"I expected a school disco," Elijah said.

"Me too," Daniel laughed. "I knew they were using the live band but didn't expect all this."

"I didn't bring my dancing shoes," Elijah said. "C'mon, let's see if we can get a drink."

The place was jammed. Rather than try to squeeze into the crowd around the circular bar, they found a spot toward the back and flagged down a waiter.

"What do you fancy?" Elijah asked.

"I've been drinking wine all night. It's time for a change. A cocktail, I think. A Tom Collins would be nice."

"Sounds good," Elijah said, ordering the same.

From the raised section at the rear, they had a great view of the main floor. The party was going strong. The company dancers moved among the tables, encouraging guests to get up and enjoy themselves. The band played *Dancing Queen* and it had the desired effect — suddenly the place was jumping.

"What are your plans when you get home?" Daniel asked. He had to stand close to Elijah to make himself heard, putting a hand on his shoulder with his mouth close to his ear. That was nothing to complain about. And the smell of him was potent stuff. Daniel breathed in deeply.

"From *Groovy Time*?" Elijah asked cheekily.

God, that smile was electrifying. "From the cruise."

"Oh, that." He rolled his eyes. "Not much. Try to write some new material and find a job. I've got a handful of gigs lined up before Christmas, but other than that, my diary looks sparse. If something doesn't materialize, I'll find myself back at sea sooner than planned."

It was crazy. That someone as talented as Elijah, and relatively well-known, should struggle to find work. But that was how it goes. Daniel had been in show business long enough to know that talent only carried someone so far. The rest was luck. It didn't matter how hard someone tried.

Daniel knew there were far better singers than himself, struggling to get a break. It was no wonder people like Terry St. King developed such fragile egos. Regardless of how long someone had been in the business, unemployment was never far away.

"Is this your first season at sea?"

Elijah nodded. "But unlikely to be my last."

"It could be worse. It's not exactly slumming it on a ship like this one."

"Believe me, I'm aware of that. As someone who's slummed it many times, I know when I'm on to a good thing. How about you? What does life have in store when you get home?"

"Panto." Daniel grinned. "In Leeds. My manager has allowed me to sail around the Med all summer and now he expects me to work."

"Who are you playing?"

"Prince Charming."

"Of course. Like you could ever be anyone else," Elijah said softly.

Their cocktails arrived. Daniel's eyes met Elijah's as they took a sip, and widened appreciatively. The taste was strong and sour, just how Daniel liked them.

The band was now singing *Love Train*, while the dancers led the audience around the room in a long conga line.

"Ah, there's my friend Anouska." Elijah pointed. "The girl with the Farrah flick."

He gestured toward a young woman with Farrah Fawcett hair, dressed in a white trouser suit. She was leading a long line of enthusiastic passengers around the bar area.

"Did you know her before you came on board?"

"Yeah, she's great. She loves all this. Oh, look about." Elijah nodded in the other direction.

Daniel turned. A second conga line was moving around the other side of the bar. "Who am I looking for?"

"See that guy over there? The skinny Barry Gibb type."

He was hard to miss. Leading the conga from the other direction was a very thin man in a huge wig. It gave his head an abnormally large appearance on his skinny frame. He stood out from the other dancers, not just because of his size. While the others wholeheartedly whipped the passengers into a state of fever, he couldn't care less. With a vacant stare and painful smile, he trudged through the motions.

"Not exactly feeling the love, is he?" Daniel said, watching with morbid interest. "Is he another friend of yours?"

"*God, no.*" Elijah grimaced. "I met him for the first time tonight." He told Daniel what had gone down in his dressing room earlier. "Can you believe it? Out of nowhere, he stumbles in and makes a proposal like that. *The best little cock sucker at sea.*"

Daniel laughed. As much as he liked Elijah, he didn't have the balls to ask him out — much less offer him a blow job. Not yet anyway. "Some people are forward like that."

"Or stoned."

"You're kidding?"

"Nope. He was off his tits. I've seen enough people under the influence to recognize a hot mess."

"What an idiot. If he's caught they'll fire him. Worse, if they find him in possession on the ship, he'll be busted."

"Exactly. I know trouble when I see it and he's it. I plan to keep well clear of him from now on."

Daniel took another look at the dancer. He passed right below where they stood, bumped into a table, spilled a few drinks and continued his conga without stopping. There was something very familiar about that face. Beneath the wig and the costume — he could swear they'd met before. He just couldn't place him.

"What did you say his name was?"

"Oliver," Elijah answered.

He looked again, harder this time. Squinting to see his face without all the distractions. Oliver? *No, it couldn't be? Was it?*

"He's not Oliver Gill, is he?"

"I didn't get his second name," Elijah said, following Daniel's gaze. "I can find out though. Anouska will know. Do you recognize him?"

"Maybe. I'm not sure."

"Who's Oliver Gill?"

"Well, we haven't actually met," Daniel said. "Not formally anyway. Our paths have crossed over the years but we've never worked together. Always a near miss."

"If the experience I had earlier is anything to go by, I'd say those were very *lucky* misses."

"Hmm." Daniel couldn't stop staring. The more he looked, the more certain he became. It *was* Oliver Gill.

"C'mon then, who is this guy?"

"I'm still not sure it's him. You know those cheesy videos you said you watched from my boyband days?"

"They're ingrained on my brain." He winked. "Never to be forgotten."

"Well, I wasn't aware of it when I auditioned, but I was a replacement singer. The boys had been together for a while when I joined. They'd recorded the album and were all set to put out the first single when they sacked the lead boy. Artistic differences, they said at the time. By all accounts he was a nightmare. He pissed off everyone – the other guys, the managers, the producers. I understand he was insufferable."

"So they gave him the boot?"

Daniel nodded. "That was Oliver Gill. When they hired me, I had five days to learn all the songs and re-record the vocals. They took his voice off the album and replaced it with mine."

"He must have been a real pain in the arse to get rid of him like that."

"Well, I never actually met him so I can't comment. They got rid of him before I started. Though none of the other guys had a good word to say about him."

"And this is him?"

"Maybe. It does look a bit like him. But that's not everything. After Overload, quite a few years later, he auditioned for *The One*. The same series I did."

"The series you won?"

"Again, we didn't actually meet. I saw him at some of the auditions but he was eliminated by the judges early on."

Elijah chuckled. "He must really love you. Taking two plum jobs from him."

"I've never done anything against him. Not personally. I was hired for Overload after he got fired. And there were thousands of contestants against me in *The One*. It was one of their biggest seasons. I wasn't aware of Oliver until the kick-off at one of the later additions."

How strange, their paths crossing once again, out here in the middle of the ocean.

* * * *

It was him all right! The sly bastard!
Who does he think he is? Staring at me like that.
Oliver could barely believe his eyes when he'd seen the smug bastard's face on Helen's computer this afternoon. The shock of that photo had been bad enough. Now the gruesome reality was staring right at him. To make it worse, he was with that sexy comedian, Elijah.

Doesn't Elijah want to get it on with me later? I thought I was on a promise. It's certainly not happening now. If Elijah was involved with Daniel Blake, he obviously had terrible taste. Oliver wanted nothing more to do with him. *The two-faced fucker.*

Daniel had lost no time. The slut had only come on board this afternoon and was already sniffing around the man Oliver had singled out for himself. Not that *that* should surprise anyone. Daniel had stolen his entire career — snatching a man was nothing in comparison.

Oliver felt sick. It was partly to do with the tremendous come-down — he'd finished the coke hours ago — and partly because of this nauseating conga he was obliged to lead. But mainly through seeing his adversary again.

The man had been a thorn in his side his whole life.

Oliver led the conga back to the dance floor. This was demeaning. Degrading himself in this tacky spectacle while Daniel was on the ship to perform a headline show. *In the fucking theater.*

It's so wrong.

It this wasn't unbearable enough already, the next song was *Night Fever. His song.* He would have killed it and shown these idiot passengers what real talent looked and sounded like.

But tonight, they had given his song to Vladislav — the

tone-deaf Russian.

It was the final indignity.

He would say his career had hit rock bottom, except it never had a chance to get started. Thanks to Daniel.

Every opportunity that ever came his way, Daniel stole it. *The bastard is pure poison.*

Vladislav took to the mic and launched into his especially flat rendition of *Night Fever*. The passengers were so drunk that none of them noticed how bad it was. They whooped and clapped along to the song. It was no better than they deserved.

Normally Oliver would have seen the funny side. He'd have laughed at the Russian's piss-poor vocals, smug in the knowledge that they'd never give him another solo. But it was too much for him to laugh tonight.

He stalked to the side of the stage, out of sight of the audience. Helen and that bastard Orestis expected him to keep dancing, to stoke the crowd while someone else murdered his song.

Not a fucking chance.

Damn, his head was pounding. He'd overdone it today. Indulged too much. He was paying for it now. Should have rationed the coke better. One more bump would have seen him through this hell.

"What are you doing here?" A voice barked in his ear. Orestis. "The show isn't over yet."

"You can't be serious," he spat back. "You want me to go out there and listen to that Russian queen destroy my song?"

"No, I expect you to be out there dancing and smiling, making sure everyone in that room has a tremendous time."

"Jesus Christ couldn't make them happy. Not when Vlad is singing. I say *singing* in the loosest sense of the word. I've heard seals bark in better tune. You really fucked up letting him take the solo."

Orestis gripped his arm and drew him closer. "Listen up, you little bitch. Your pissy attitude is getting on my last nerve. I already intend to make sure you never work on another Royal Atlantic liner. If you don't want me to ensure you're blacklisted from all major cruise ships, get your scrawny ass on the floor and dance."

"You can't do that," Oliver shrieked. He was less certain than he sounded. He didn't know what kind of influence Orestis had.

"Try me. One false step from you between here and Southampton and you're finished. Now get on that fucking floor and do what we pay you to do."

The temptation to tell him exactly where to stick his lousy cruise ship was near overwhelming but Oliver had burned too many bridges already. He needed this and any subsequent job he could get hold of. So he went back to the dance floor with a rictus smile plastered across his face. He booty bumped some two-ton heifer in a floral blouse and cream linen trousers that showed every cottage cheese dimple on her arse. Vladislav failed to hit the final top note and the hell was over.

Helen came on the mic to keep the audience geared up. "Weren't they marvelous, ladies and gentlemen? C'mon, big round of applause if you enjoyed that party."

There was more insane grinning and clapping. A last refrain of *Night Fever*. The heifer tried to get him to dance with her again but Oliver was already gone.

What a fucking night. The worst thing he'd ever experienced since boarding this floating buffet carriage.

At least he could go to bed now. He wasn't even interested in pursuing Elijah. He was no great loss. Anyway, the last thing he felt like was sex. His butthole was raw. Those filthy foreigners had taken it out of him this afternoon.

If Elijah had been a little nicer to him, more worthy, he might have mustered some enthusiasm for a fuck or one of his special blow jobs. But there was no chance of that now. Elijah could stick it to Daniel, who by all accounts was a totally boring fuck. Oliver had no reason to doubt those rumors—he'd started them himself. Everything about

Daniel was boring—it stood to reason he'd be terrible in the sack too.

"Wot a night. 'Effin' brilliant." Shanitta was at his side, out of breath. Sweat glistened on top of her heavy stage makeup. She wore a purple halter-neck top and Liza Minelli wig. "Wot's wrong with your face? You look like someone took a shit in your shoe." She cackled at her own wit.

"I'm sick of this damn ship and being treated like a cunt the whole the time."

"It's not that bad. You're on a come-down, babe. That's all. Told you not to get too wired today. Chill."

Poor, clueless Shanitta. This was a big deal for her. She's never known the upper reaches of fame. The intrigue and glamour that went with it. She'd never got out of the chorus and never would. Silly cow.

Around them, the Sky Lounge was winding down. The band packed away their gear while the passengers filtered off. Some of them would head to bed, some would be off to stuff their faces in Cafe24, while others moved down to the lower decks, where the late-night party would continue in the martini bar, the casino and Jimmy's Night Club.

"Fancy a drink in the mess?" Shanitta asked.

"I'm going to bed," he sulked.

"Have a night cap. One for the road."

"Oh, all right. Twist my arm. But just one."

Shanitta's 'ones for the road' had a habit of becoming six or seven.

They were moving toward the crew door when he heard hasty footsteps coming up behind. *This had better not be another moronic passenger,* he thought. The loser probably wanted a selfie.

"Excuse me." It was a man's voice. He recognized it straight away. "It's Oliver, isn't it?"

Oh God, no. No.

Oliver turned, stony faced.

Daniel Blake had always been a good-looking shit. Oliver hated him but had to admit he was a looker. Even more so in the flesh. He felt his heart give a little quiver as they came face to face. Even his own body was betraying him.

Daniel smiled, so brilliantly that it almost melted Oliver's icy core. But not quite.

"My word, it is you," Daniel enthused. He grabbed Oliver's hand and shook it. His grip was very strong, very dry. "It's Daniel Blake."

"Hi." Oliver raised an insincere smile.

"Oh, my God, do you two know each other?" Shanitta butted in. "Daniel, I love you. I used to have your CD. It was mint, man."

"We were never formally introduced," Daniel said. "We've kind of moved around each other for years without meeting properly. You know what it's like. Going after the same jobs. But it's nice to meet you at last. After all these years. Wow."

Am I hearing this bullshit? Oliver couldn't take the nerve of this twat.

"That's an interesting way of looking at things," Oliver said. "Through rose-tinted lenses, you could say."

"Babes," Shanitta put a taloned hand on his arm. "Rude."

"Not really," Oliver said. "You see, I *had* a job once upon a time. I was the lead singer in a band. A boy band. We were good. Going places. Tipped for the big time and all that."

The smile faded from Daniel's face. *Good.* Oliver was beginning to enjoy himself.

"We were managed by this sleazy old queen. Sam LeFerve, a real fat bastard. Always seeking to get his hands on my dick. I was a cute little thing in my teens. But I wouldn't give it up. Didn't have to, because I knew I had talent. Sam cared little for talent so he sacked me and replaced me with a boy who was a bit more…easy."

He tipped his head toward Daniel to make his point.

Daniel looked incredulous. "Oliver, you've got it all wrong. That's not what went on."

"Isn't it? A pretty accurate summary in my opinion," he sneered. "Of course, it didn't do them much good. Sam might have got his pedo hands on some underage cock but the band was a flop. A huge flop! And it was more than they deserved because they were shit."

Daniel gawped at him. "Oliver, I... I..."

Oliver raised his hand in Daniel's face. "*Whatever.* You've got some balls, I'll give you that. Waltzing over and expecting me to kiss your arse. Believe me, sweetie, that's never going to happen. I might not have been as fortunate as you but I didn't have to screw my way to the top. And you did teach me something all those years ago. It's a lesson I've always been grateful for and have never ignored. *Trust no bitch.*"

Daniel took a step back, both hands raised. "Oliver, c'mon. Why don't we have a drink together, somewhere quiet? There seem to be some misunderstandings we should put right."

"Trust. No. Bitch," Oliver repeated slowly. "It's become my motto and it's served me well. You can have that drink alone and I dearly hope you choke on it. Now get out of my face."

"*Oliver,*" Shanitta gasped.

He was already on his way, through the staff door and along the corridor. The look of horror on Daniel's face as he left was priceless. Oliver wished he'd said more. Maybe he would.

It would be another two days until they reached England. He could cause a lot of trouble if he wanted to.

For the first time all night he had something to smile about.

* * * *

Elijah walked the top deck of the ship with Daniel. It was a breezy night but far from unpleasant. The sky above was pure black. Daniel had been quiet since coming back. Elijah had tried to warn him that Oliver was unlikely to accept an olive branch. He didn't strike Elijah as the type. Vicious, bitchy, cunty — all those things. He would bear a grudge for sure. But accepting the hand of friendship from an enemy? No chance.

He knew from the sad expression on Daniel's face that he'd been right. Elijah's heart was heavy for him. Daniel meant well. They had only just met but he knew instinctively that he was a nice guy. Not just nice. He was probably the loveliest man he'd ever met.

"How about a breath of air?" Elijah suggested. "It'll blow the bullshit away."

They walked the entire starboard side before Elijah asked, "How did it go?"

Daniel's sigh was carried on the sea breeze. "He hates me."

"Haters gonna hate," Elijah drawled.

Daniel turned to look at him. His eyes sparkled in the deck lights and his soft hair was ruffled by the wind. Elijah felt like the floor had dropped beneath his feet. He was falling hard.

"He thinks I seduced the band manager so I could take his place."

"You schemer," Elijah said in mock shock. "So who did you screw to get him kicked off *The One*?"

Daniel snorted softly. "We didn't get that far. But I'm sure it was something terribly evil."

"I'd be very disappointed if it wasn't. He'd have won the hearts of the nation if it wasn't for you."

"No doubt about it."

"Ah, fuck 'em," Elijah said. "You tried to be nice and he doesn't want to know. It's his loss, not yours. Don't let it fester."

They reached the stern. Below them, a great wake cut across the inky black water. They leaned against the rail, side by side, and breathed in the salty air. Maybe it was the night or the ocean, the freshness of the breeze, but Elijah realized right there how easy it would be to fall in love with Daniel. How close he was to it already.

He was alone at sea with the most handsome man he had ever met.

"This is what it's all about," Daniel said, gazing out into the night.

"It sure is. I don't think I'll ever get tired of it."

Elijah moved closer to him. Their hips were lightly touching. He noticed that Daniel didn't pull away. The contact was barely there but it was enough — he could feel the warmth of Daniel's body through it.

Elijah was conflicted. Why did he have to sleep with Vladislav last night? And fuck him again this morning. If only he'd known he was going to meet Daniel today.

He wanted him with every fiber of his body. His heart ached and his stomach churned. His cock was in a state of arousal — it had been for most of the night. His balls were tight with tension. God, he was on fire.

But it just wasn't right tonight. He couldn't do it — wouldn't do it — not so soon after the Russian. Daniel was too special for that.

He deserved so much better.

Daniel moved closer, pressing more firmly against his hip. He put his arm around Elijah's waist. Elijah couldn't help himself and did the same. Daniel's waist was firm beneath his palm. They stood together, not talking, quietly watching the wake of the ship.

There was no pressure from either of them.

For tonight, this was enough.

There would be plenty of time in the coming days to take things further.

Chapter Eight

On Friday morning, the *Atlantic Anthem* cleared the northern coast of Spain and entered the Bay of Biscay, a notorious area in the North East Atlantic for its unpredictable weather and high seas. Conditions were favorable that morning, with clear skies and only moderate winds. The waves reached an average height of nine feet. Though the ship pitched a little more than usual, it was relatively minor for a vessel of its size and ability and the passengers and crew experienced little discomfort.

Despite going to bed late, Daniel was awake at seven. It had been a troubled night. The scene with Oliver Gill in the Sky Lounge played on a perpetual loop in his mind. From the moment he put his head down, it was all he could think about.

Oliver hated him. He couldn't have made that more obvious. Did he honestly believe all the things he'd said? That Daniel had slept with Sam, their manager, to steal his position in Overload? That was insane. Sam was loud, brash — outright rude most of the time — but he hadn't once made a pass at him.

Daniel eventually got sick of turning the same events over in his mind and got out of bed. He couldn't squander energy on this. Not on show day. He needed to concentrate. There was rehearsal with the band this morning and two hour-long sets this evening. He had to deliver.

He put on shorts, running shoes, T-shirt and a baseball cap. Exercise. That would erase those negative thoughts and focus his mind on more essential matters.

He was intent on hitting the gym until he reached the top

level. It was a fine morning with blue skies and fresh sea air. Eschewing the air-conditioned comfort of the gym, he set off jogging around the deck. This early in the day, there were few people about, just a couple of other runners. It was the ideal time to make a few laps of the track.

Thoughts of Oliver weren't that easy to shake. The hate in his eyes when he'd unleashed his venom last night. Daniel wasn't familiar with such spite. He was used to bitchiness, jealousy too, but what he'd seen in Oliver was something more malignant. Toxic. Was there anything he could do to change his mind? To convince him of what really happened. Would it matter?

It was worth a try.

After five laps of the deck, he forced himself to think about something else. The set list for his show was already decided. There was nothing he could add—it would come together when he ran it with the band. Music was a collaboration. It came alive with other people. The musicians and the audience.

His thoughts turned to Elijah.

Now there was an unexpected distraction. Until the uproar with Oliver, last night had been just about perfect, thanks to Elijah. And after all that crap with Oliver, it had been rescued with a kiss.

Elijah was a beautiful man. Not just physically. He was a nice, warm-hearted and genuinely funny guy. Men like that were hard to find—the complete package.

Still, Daniel realized, he had to be careful. This wasn't the time to fall in love, much less the place. On a ship, with only two days left of the journey. Come Sunday, they would go their separate ways. There was no future in that.

Does there have to be?

They were grown men after all. Single with no ties or responsibilities. Couldn't they just enjoy the next two days and leave it there? It was a tempting idea. Perhaps *too* tempting.

Could he really hold his feelings in check and say goodbye

as surely as that? Without feeling any regret? Without getting hurt?

Not likely. Daniel knew himself better than that. He was not the love 'em and leave 'em type. And Elijah was not the kind of man he could easily let go of. They would both get hurt.

It was better to leave things as they were. Friendly. Uninvolved. Uncomplicated. He was here to do a job. That was what he should focus on.

* * * *

Oliver woke up in his bunk with a bad head and an even worse mood. For a few hungover moments, he dared to believe that yesterday had been nothing but a drug-induced fever dream. A delirious nightmare from start to finish. It was a nice thought and he clung to it for as long as possible.

Until the overweight bastard in the bunk beneath him let out a ripe fart and turned over to waft the covers.

It was real all right. Every hideous minute of it.

The last few hours were a bit sketchy. He recalled going to the crew bar with Shanitta after his run in with Daniel – the arrogant arsehole. He remembered drinking vodka shots and telling anyone who would listen what a talentless slut Daniel was. A slut who had stolen every decent opportunity that had ever come Oliver's way.

Oh yes, he'd left them in no doubt about the kind of man Daniel was.

By two he'd been on a roll and it had been Vladislav's turn. Oliver informed the morose Russian, in very clear terms, what a terrible singer he was. Not just that. *'Elijah Mann must have the worst taste in men. Fucking you one night, then picking up that awful cabaret crooner the next. He must be blind and deaf.'*

Oh yes, Oliver chuckled into his pillow. *That was fun.* The look on Vlad's face had been priceless. Almost as satisfying as Daniel's stunned mullet expression when he'd told him what he thought of him. There were a few small pleasures left in the world and being rude to stupid people was one of the best.

The stink from the bunk below hit his nostrils and forced him out of bed.

"For fuck's sake. What crawled up your arse and died?"

He snatched a bottle of Beckham cologne from the dresser and sprayed the cabin.

"Knock it off." The heap in the bunk pulled the covers over his head. "That stuff stinks."

"Not as much as your filthy hole," Oliver snapped, stumbling into the bathroom.

Oh Jesus, his head. No, his whole body. He hurt all over. It didn't help that the fucking ship was rocking like a toy in this bastard ocean. How rough was it out there this morning? Not as rough as he felt in here.

He sat down to pee, resting his head on the cool shower cubicle, and let out a low groan.

"Let me die. Anything would be better than this."

"Just do it quietly," shouted the voice from the bedroom.

"Screw you, lard arse."

Overload. What a talentless bunch of losers they were. It had been obvious to Oliver from the very beginning that the band was going nowhere. He'd hated being a member of a boyband. It had been only a means to an end. A stepping stone to fame. He had always intended to ditch the other four once they'd gained a bit of publicity.

Oliver dreamed of being a solo artist, not the talented one in a crappy five-piece lineup.

It had been an indignity having to share the stage with those idiots. They'd looked like shit and sounded worse. And the music had been dire. He'd pleaded with the producers every day to take the others off the record and only use his vocals.

'It'll sound so much better,' he'd said repeatedly.

It had been a waste of breath.

Sam LeFerve, the fat fuck manager, had taken him into

his office after a noisy outburst in the studio one day.

'You've got some attitude, kid,' Sam said. 'And it stinks. I've got a lot of money invested in this project and you're a liability I can do without. I hate to do this but it's over. You're fired.'

'What!' He heard the words but couldn't believe them. 'You can't sack me. I'm the lead singer. You need to get rid of the others.'

Sam shook his head. 'I've got no problem with the other boys. They look good and they do what they're told to. You're a pain in the arse I just don't need.'

Oliver trembled. Sam was serious. Shit! Why couldn't he have kept his mouth shut? 'Listen, I'm sorry. Okay? I'll keep quiet from now on. Do what you say.'

'I'm sorry but it's over. There's no place for you in this band.'

'There's no place for you in this band.'

Twelve years later, those words still smarted. The pain and the indignity were just as fresh as the day Sam booted him out.

Sam LeFerve was a bastard. They were all bastards. Every single one of the fuckers involved in the Overload shit-fest.

Now the biggest bastard was here, on board the ship, threatening to steal glory from him again. Daniel Blake. The greatest shit of all. The no-talent twink who'd ousted him in a crappy boy band.

It hadn't done them much good at the time. Daniel had re-recorded all his vocals on the Overload album but the band was still a gigantic flop. They'd been out on their arses within a year, dropped by Sam when they failed to hit big. All five of those losers — fired.

It was some consolation. It would have been better if Oliver had made it as a solo artist while Overload bombed, but that didn't materialize. Daniel Blake had seen to that again.

The slimy motherfucking son of a bitch had been there every time Oliver's career had taken off. He was like a show-business grim reaper, arriving at every opportunity Oliver was given—killing his dreams stone dead.

Not this time.

Revenge. It had been a long time coming. Now, with two days at sea ahead of them, Oliver would finally have it.

Daniel Blake would pay big for everything he'd done.

* * * *

Elijah decided to take a walk. He felt wonderful as soon as he woke up. There was no hangover, despite the cocktails he'd enjoyed with Daniel last night. *Daniel.* Just thinking about him made him smile.

He couldn't get him out of his head. He'd been thinking about him when he fell asleep and he was the very first thought when his eyes opened this morning. And he had dreamed about him all night in between. He hadn't been this wrapped up in a man in a long time. Such a rapid infatuation. It wasn't his style.

And that kiss. Oh God, to have more of that.

Showered and refreshed, he put on chinos and a short-sleeved shirt. The ship was bouncing lightly on the swell but after a minute on the balcony, under clear blue skies, he realized it was going to be a beautiful day.

When he returned to England on Sunday, winter would be approaching. The best thing to do today was make the most of the weather while it lasted. Starting with a walk before breakfast.

He left his stateroom and headed for the upper decks. He had a marvelous feel for today. He was going to enjoy it. No work, no responsibilities. He could sit back and enjoy whatever came his way. And he had Daniel's show to look forward to later. He was already excited about that.

Elijah didn't have to wait that long. As he strode on deck and inhaled the salty air, the man who dominated all his thoughts came running toward him. In shorts and a baseball cap, dripping with sweat, he was still drop-dead gorgeous. Those strong, hairy calves and the bulge in the front of those shorts. He was too damn perfect.

Daniel spotted him at the same time and altered course, ambling toward him with a wide smile.

"Hey."

"Hi." Elijah grinned. "You must be committed, working out this early. I feel like a sloth now."

Daniel took off his cap. His hair was wet and soaked flat to his head. Beads of sweat rolled down his brow. He mopped it against his forearm. "This isn't normal. I was awake early and couldn't sleep. I thought it was better to do something productive with my time than lie in bed doing nothing."

"There I figured I was being good, taking a walk before breakfast."

"It's your day off, isn't it? You can do whatever you like. I would if I were you."

Elijah felt it all over again—that sucker punch—his head, his heart, his stomach. Each time he saw Daniel he experienced it anew. However much he thought about him, nothing compared to the physical and emotional reaction that occurred when they met.

I'm falling in love with him. That's impossible, he told himself, *you hardly know him.* It didn't matter. This was something out of his control. These feelings—they were unstoppable.

"I…had a nice time last night," Elijah said.

"I did too," Daniel replied. "Maybe a cocktail too many, but I don't feel too bad for it this morning."

After the kiss in the moonlight, they'd continued to the martini bar on Deck Four. They'd had another Tom Collins before switching to vodka martinis. The time had flown until Daniel had called a halt at two o'clock. He had two shows the next day and couldn't stay up drinking all night, enticing as that was.

"Would you like to have breakfast? You haven't eaten already, have you?"

"I haven't," Daniel answered. "But I'm not really dressed for it. Not even for Cafe24. I stink."

His T-shirt, bathed in sweat, stuck to his torso. Elijah took in the broad span of his chest, the hard, excited tips of his nipples.

"You look good enough to me." The words cascaded from his mouth unchecked.

Daniel laughed and sweet patches of red colored his cheeks. He looked even more adorable when he blushed.

"Sorry," Elijah said.

"Don't be," Daniel replied, tenderly patting his shoulder. "Can you hold on fifteen minutes? Give me time for a swift shower and a change of clothes."

"Absolutely. I want to take that walk I promised myself."

"Okay." Daniel grinned. "I'll see you here in fifteen. Won't be long."

* * * *

They were just ahead of the breakfast rush, securing a prime ocean view table. In fifteen minutes, Daniel had transformed himself. His brown hair was washed and soft, bare of any fussy product. He wore a white linen shirt and cream chinos. His skin shone, enlivened by the exercise.

He ate a simple breakfast of scrambled eggs, grilled mushrooms and toast with apple juice and tea. Elijah went for a continental option of cured meats, cheese and fruit, orange juice and coffee. For once the food wasn't important—it was the company that mattered more.

"All set for your shows?" he asked.

"Pretty much," Daniel said, criss-crossing ketchup over his eggs. "I've got a run through with the band at eleven. It's tight. Ninety-minute rehearsal for a one hour show. We'll only get one crack at each song."

"Those guys work hard."

"Don't they just. But they also work fast. I'm not concerned. I've worked with them before. They'll pick this up in no time at all. Besides, it requires us to work harder on the night—being under-rehearsed, not too polished. I like that."

"Me too," Elijah said. He found it hard to concentrate on breakfast. All he wanted to do was stare at Daniel. His eyes, his mouth, his hands. He turned him on without trying. Beneath the table, Elijah was concealing a huge boner. "I can't wait to hear you sing. I've seen you on TV loads, but watching you live, that will be something else."

"I love doing the live shows," Daniel said. "For some singers, it's all about TV and the exposure it brings, but for me, it's the stage. That's where it really happens."

"I know what you mean."

Daniel took a sip of juice, watching Elijah with level, blue eyes. Just like last night, conversation came easily between them. They talked about work and travel, about music and books and movies they loved.

It was nice. Breakfast with Daniel. Elijah could get used to it. The empty plates were cleared away. Their drinks were almost finished but neither of them was in a hurry to move. Elijah was afraid that getting up from the table would break the spell.

The spell of love? It surely felt like it. He had to remind himself again. *This love stuff is crazy. Knock it off.*

The mood was broken by the appearance of Helen McDonald. The entertainment manager stood over their table, engulfing them in a cloud of sweet perfume.

"Guys, guys, I'm so glad to catch you together." Helen was oblivious to the fact that she might be interrupting.

"Morning, Helen," they said in near unison.

"Can you spare half an hour this morning? I'd like you both to attend my morning meeting with the entertainment crew. So we can get a hold on tomorrow night's finale. It's not just the last show of the cruise but the last show of the maiden season. It's got to be special — amazing — and I want you guys to play a big part in that."

"What time do you want us?" Daniel asked.

"The meeting starts in five minutes but you don't need to be there for that. It won't be relevant. Come down for ten-thirty, we'll talk about the finale then. Yes?"

With that, she was gone, leaving a wake of perfume behind her.

Their eyes met again and they both laughed.

"I guess that's the end of breakfast," Elijah said.

"So much for your day off too," Daniel said as they left the restaurant. "But I did enjoy that."

"Me too," Elijah said. He meant it. He was happy. Happier than he had been in a long time and Daniel was the reason for it, the sole reason. Suddenly he felt inspired. Outside the restaurant, as they were walking toward the lift, he placed a hand on Daniel's arm. "Let's go outside for a minute. There's something I want to say."

Daniel looked at him. His blue eyes were dazzling. An uncertain smile hovered on his lips.

They walked onto the deck. The sun still shone and a fresh wind pulled at their hair. Elijah's pulse raced. His insides were in knots.

"Look, Daniel, this might sound weird, especially as we only met yesterday. But we have so little time and I…well, I don't want to squander it. If I've got any of this wrong please say so and I'll shut my stupid mouth right up."

They leaned against the rail. Daniel stepped close. "I think I know what you're going to say. I'm listening."

Elijah exhaled. Every part of him was tense. "I like you a lot. Like is the wrong word because it's more than that, but I can't think of anything more appropriate right now. Oh God, I'm rambling and I didn't want to do that."

"It's okay," Daniel said softly. "And I feel the same way too."

Elijah was shaking. "You do?"

"Absolutely. Last night. The kiss. Isn't it obvious?"

"Oh, thank God," he said, immediate relieved. He hadn't fucked this up. "So what are we gonna do about it?"

"Well." Daniel smiled. "You said it yourself, we don't have the luxury of time to waste."

Suddenly brave, Elijah took his hand. "You've got a full

day today. Rehearsals, two shows—I don't want to get in the way of that. But as soon as you come off stage this evening—how about we get together properly? For a date."

Daniel smiled widely. *Oh God, that smile*. It rocked him to the core.

"A date?"

"A real date. The two of us. No singers. No seventies dancers. No disco. Just the two of us."

"It sounds perfect in every way but one."

"What's that?"

"Tonight is a long way off."

"It is, isn't it?"

Their mouths came closer, closer. The kiss was long and sweet, their tongues tentatively touching. Elijah reacted with his entire body.

Eventually they broke apart, smiling.

Elijah's lips tingled.

"That's enough to get me through the day," Daniel said. "That and the thought of going on a date with you."

"Until tonight then."

"Until tonight."

Chapter Nine

Helen McDonald ran a tight department. She had to. If she allowed her staff an inch of slack they would use it to string her up. They had plenty to say behind her back. She wasn't stupid. It was part of being the boss. Being liked didn't come into it. She wanted work to be an agreeable experience for everyone, including herself, and she tried to be fair.

Terry St. King thought she had discriminated against him by booking Daniel for the Saturday matinee. He was wrong. Helen was accountable to the captain, the company and the passengers. She based her decisions on information drawn from all three sources. Fact—Terry was not as popular as he thought he was.

He was a niche entertainer. In the confines of the Moonlight Lounge, he was perfect. Those passengers who enjoyed his antiquated act—the oldest five percent—could find him there. But he was all wrong for the main stage. Whenever he played a headliner, the feedback was dreadful. The majority of passengers didn't want to see or hear him. His geriatric groupies would fill up the first three rows and give each song a standing ovation, which inflated his already grand ego, but farther back the seats were always empty. Those who came out of morbid curiosity rarely stayed for the end.

Helen shielded him from the worst of the criticism. Maybe that was her mistake, allowing his ego to get out of hand.

"Seeing how you've stolen my matinee and handed it to that fluffy little boy-toy, the least you can do is let me top the bill in the finale."

Terry's droning voice had dominated the last five minutes

of the morning meeting. Terry rarely attended these staff briefings. Only when he wanted to make a point. Around the table sat the dancers, band leader, stage manager, singers and production heads. None of them were listening and private conversations had broken out.

"No one is topping the bill," Helen said firmly, lifting her voice to bring the meeting back to order. "The finale is an ensemble effort."

Terry didn't give in so easily. "But you know very well my audience won't leave the ship until they've seen me play the main stage. Do you want to face a mutiny?"

As sniggers rippled around the room, Helen struggled to retain her patience.

"They see you every night of the cruise."

"But not on the main stage," he said forcefully. "That pokey lounge is not the same thing."

Bloody performers. She'd been a singer herself and had never been as much trouble as this lot. She doubted Maria Callas had been so demanding.

"All right," she sighed. "You can have one song."

"Oh, no," he simpered triumphantly. "I'll need three to do the show justice."

"You've got one," she said resolutely. "And make certain it's something upbeat and relatively modern. None of your old war-time hits. I want this to be a party."

"But *The Long and the Short and the Tall* is my standard. An absolute fan favorite."

"No, do *Copacabana*." She turned to the company dancers. "Get together with Terry and prepare a routine. I want a full production number for this."

"Oh, come on," Anouska Frost complained. "We've got enough going on without having to fit that in."

"Yeah," Shanitta chipped in. "Why do we 'ave to carry the old bleeder?"

Terry glared. "This old bleeder was performing for royalty before you were even thought of, you ungrateful twat." He pronounced it 'tw-art'.

"Enough," Helen snapped. "Just do what you're told, all of you. Or no one will be in the finale."

"Hang on," Oliver Gill spoke up.

Until that moment Helen thought he'd been asleep. He was near comatose. In a scruffy T-shirt and shorts, with dark sunken eyes and waxy skin, he looked a mess.

"What is it, Oliver?"

"How come he gets a solo spot and I don't? You promised me a headliner and that hasn't come through. The least you can do is give me a solo in the finale. You owe me big time."

Helen looked desperately at Orestis, her right-hand man.

"We owe you nothing. And there are no more solos," the director said emphatically. "And after last night's performance, Oliver, you're lucky to still be here. See me in my office after this meeting."

Oliver looked daggers at Helen and Orestis but wisely kept his mouth shut. Terry stared smugly at the younger man but said nothing. Thank God the season was almost over. Helen was badly in need of a break. She'd had to manage an exceptionally difficult bunch this year. Maybe she was getting too old for all this drama. Maybe not.

Maybe they were just arseholes.

Next season, she'd make certain she got a more professional team.

There was a knock at the door and it opened. It was Daniel and Elijah.

"Are you ready for us now?" Daniel asked.

"Absolutely. Come in boys, take a seat." What she wouldn't do to get this pair on her permanent staff. Smart, good-looking, polite, professional and talented, they were the complete package. Both of them. That was so hard to find.

"I understood this was a *staff* meeting," Terry said slyly.

He had a nerve, given how few he'd attended himself.

"I invited Daniel and Elijah," she said. "They're the guest performers in tomorrow's program. I want to make sure that we all know what we're doing."

"Welcome, guys, great to see you here," Anouska beamed. With Helen and Orestis, she was the only other person at the table to look happy about their inclusion.

"I really think the passengers would appreciate it more if the finale was kept exclusively to crew members," Terry sneered. "On a two-week cruise we become like family to them. They want to say a proper goodbye to us."

This insufferable old shit didn't know when to quit. "You think wrong, Terry," Helen said. "That's not the way we work and you know it. The finale has always been a variety show comprising crew and guest artists."

"I think it would be better if it was just us," Terry said, preening.

"It wouldn't."

Daniel and Elijah looked awfully uneasy, sitting together at the top of the table. Maybe it hadn't been such a great idea to invite them. She should have known this lot would be jealous. They didn't bat an eye when she brought Blackpool-style cabaret acts, aging magicians or out-of-date comedians into the finale. But these two, with their talent and TV profile, were bound to ruffle a few feathers.

"Welcome, boys, both of you," she said warmly. "It's a pleasure to have you here and I know the passengers will appreciate another chance to see you." She made a point of turning her attention back to the table. "If you didn't have time to see him last night, Elijah went down a storm in the theater. People were still coming up to me at breakfast to say how great he was. He's the talk of the ship. He's marvelous, he really is."

That wiped some of the smug expressions from their faces.

"Please," Elijah said. "You're making me blush."

"Don't be modest. You deserve every bit of it. The audience loved your show and that's what we're all here for. To give them a good time."

"I do my best," he said.

"So here's what I was thinking for tomorrow. We'll open

with a tremendous number from the house singers and dancers. Then I'll chat to the crowd and do a song of my own. Another group routine, then Terry will do a song, and after that I figured you, Elijah, could come on and do a routine. Does ten minutes sound okay?"

"Not a problem," he said. "I'll prepare a couple of gags but mostly I'll spar off the audience and get a rapport going. That kind of stuff works best."

Helen couldn't help smiling. What a delight it was to ask somebody to do something and hear their enthusiasm for it. No whining. No bitching. No excuses. There would definitely be some changes around here next season. More of Elijah's attitude and lot less of Terry and Oliver. The wannabe divas could find another ship to lord it over.

"Great stuff. And right after Elijah's piece, I thought Daniel could come in. I know you've already got a show in the afternoon and I don't want to burden you, but could you do two, maybe three songs in the evening?"

"*Three!*" Terry squealed. "And I only get one?"

"That's what I said."

Daniel looked embarrassed. *Poor boy.* She shouldn't have put him in this position. These green-eyed bitches were too much.

"Well, er" — Daniel looked uncertainly between Helen and Terry — "three songs is okay with me. How does one ballad and two upbeat numbers sound?"

"Perfect."

"I've got a practice run with the band right after this meeting," he said. "I'll work something out with them and get back to you."

"Excellent," she enthused. "After you, I'll come back on to wish everyone a safe journey home, then you'll all join me for the closing number *That's What Friends Are For*. So, we all know what we're doing?"

There were nods and noises of assent all round the table.

"One more matter before you go." Helen picked up a memo. "It's a message from Captain Rassimov. I wanted to wait till everyone was here before delivering it. This affects all of us and it concerns the weather. The further North we go, the worse it's going to get. Swells and wind are expected to pick up this afternoon, but it's tonight and tomorrow that will really be bad."

"Great end to the season," someone said. "Sailing into a storm."

"North Biscay and the English Channel are forecast to get it bad. We're going to sail a little way out to avoid the worst of the weather in Biscay, but there's no way we can dodge the Channel. So be careful up on those stages. Safety first. Look out for each other. Don't take any risks. If the weather gets too rough, I will step in and stop the show." She turned to Daniel. "The ship may do a bit of rolling when you're up there tonight. Will you be okay?"

He nodded. "I'll be fine. I've got good sea legs. Don't worry."

"Okay. Well, it's just a precaution. A new ship like this can handle anything the ocean throws at it, but be vigilant all the same. I don't want anyone getting hurt."

* * * *

Band rehearsal went as well as Daniel expected. He'd worked with all the musicians before and they picked up his songs with ease. It helped that two of the guys had played in his touring band and knew what he wanted better than anyone.

Time was tight but they made the best of it. They ran through the songs he wanted to do that night. It was perfect despite all the distractions going on around them. Top of that list was Terry St. King, who sat in the front row of the stalls for the entire run through, arms and legs folded, lips pursed.

Daniel could have asked him to leave but didn't want to give him that satisfaction.

'You won't even know I'm here,' Terry had said as they'd

prepared for the first song. *'I won't be able to watch tonight as I have my own show, but I would regret it forever more if I didn't find out what all the fuss is about.'*

I'll show you what the fuss is all about.

Daniel was tempted to invite Terry to his Saturday matinee. He knew he had nothing better to do then, but resisted the temptation. Why stoop to Terry's level and trade insults? Instead he gave him the full works. Where he would typically hold something back during rehearsal, he went all out, giving it the full show performance.

Terry's expression became even sourer as the set rolled on. Halfway through Daniel realized that Terry wasn't alone in the auditorium. Several rows back he caught Oliver's gaunt face, staring emotionlessly toward the stage.

This must be my lucky day, he thought. *The fan club is in the house.*

He carried on undeterred, singing richer and stronger because they were there. They couldn't bring him down today, whatever storm of shit they were trying to brew up. Not after breakfast with Elijah. Not with so much to look forward to.

Sorry, fellows, if you're hoping to see me tumble, it's not going to happen.

Daniel was more disturbed by Oliver's attitude toward him than Terry's bitchiness. There was no need for them to be enemies. What had transpired in the past was nobody's fault. Daniel had known nothing of Oliver's dismissal when he'd auditioned for Overload. There had been other jobs over the years, most notably *The One*, but again, Daniel had no influence on who went through and who didn't. All he did was sing his best.

That was what he would give today and for every other performance he did on this ship – his best.

At the end of the session, the band came over to shake his hand and congratulate him.

"Shit, man, you really went for it there."

"Never heard anyone kill it like that in a run-through."

"The audience won't know what's hit them tonight."

Daniel glanced back into the auditorium. Terry and Oliver were gone. *Pity.* He'd have liked another opportunity to speak with Oliver. To try to straighten out last night's mess. It was probably just as well. He was tired and needed to save his energy for his gigs. Another tirade from Oliver would cause unnecessary stress.

He didn't need it. Today was a good one and he intended to keep it that way.

The central parade was busy as he headed out of the theater. Only a couple of days remained of the cruise and the weather on deck was not as hot as it had been. Many people were taking the moment to grab some last-minute presents and souvenirs to take home. The shops, cafes and bars were all busy.

As he stepped around the outskirts of the crowd he was spotted by Julieann, the fourteen-year-old English girl he'd met the day before.

"Oh my God, I'm sooooo excited about tonight," she squealed. Julieann was dressed in a summery top and patterned shorts. Her wild hair tumbled around her flushed face.

"That's good to hear." Daniel smiled at her. "I can't wait either. We're good to go, just waiting for show time."

"I'm going to get there extra early to secure a good seat." She produced a small notebook with the *Atlantic Anthem* logo on the front. "I bought this. Can I have your autograph?"

"Of course you can." He took her notebook and pen.

"I'm making this into an autograph book. Yours will be the first entry."

Daniel wrote,

To Julieann, may this be the first of many in your collection. Love Daniel Blake xxx.

Her eyes widened as he handed it back.

"You know, if you keep your eyes open, there's another celebrity on board. A famous comedian. I think he'd be a great addition to your book."

"Who?" she asked breathlessly.

"Elijah Mann. He did the main show last night. Did you see him?"

"No. My parents wouldn't let me go. They said it might be rude, so we went to see Terry St. King instead. Sooooo boring."

"Ooh, bad call."

"I know, right. So, is Elijah, like, famous?"

"He is. He's been on TV. Had his own show and everything. He's handsome too. I think you'll like him."

"I saw his picture in yesterday's itinerary. He did look pretty lush. I've got to find him. Thanks, Daniel. If you see him first, tell him I'm looking for him."

Daniel chuckled as Julieann hurried away. If she didn't catch Elijah herself, he would fix her up after the show tonight.

As he walked along the parade, there was an amiable atmosphere among the passengers. It was quite noticeable. Their holiday might be coming to an end but it wasn't over yet. Plenty of fun still to be had. Not just for the guests but him too.

That fun presented itself sooner than he expected when he saw Elijah sitting just inside one of the bars. He was alone. Absorbed with a Kindle, he didn't notice Daniel outside.

Daniel paused for a moment, enjoying the thrill of watching him unseen.

His bottom lip protruded slightly and his brow furrowed as he read. Daniel had never seen him so serious. On TV, he'd only ever watched his comedy stuff, never the dramatic roles he had mentioned, the terrorists and villains he got to play. It suited him. A lot. Looking so moody and intent.

Daniel was struck once more by just how attractive Elijah was. It was more than beauty because it went deeper than the skin. There was something in the core of Elijah that pulled at Daniel like a magnet.

It almost overwhelmed him.

He hadn't intended to see him again until their date tonight.

Why hang on until after the shows?

Their time was limited already.

Daniel wanted him now. To hell with waiting.

He walked into the bar.

Elijah seemed to sense his approach and looked up from his Kindle. The serious expression vanished in a second. The handsome smile that he knew so well was back.

"Hey, I thought you were working."

That smile. That voice.

"All done," Daniel said, sitting at the table.

"How was it?"

"Good, I think. My two biggest fans decided to sit in but they didn't put me off."

Elijah's brow knitted. "Fans?"

"Oliver and Terry."

He grimaced. "That's a gruesome twosome."

Daniel laughed. Elijah made him feel instantly better. To see the possibilities in everything. His gaze dropped below the smile, to the open neck of his shirt. He remembered the chest and torso he'd seen in the dressing room last night. The firm flesh, the dark hair, the hard nipples. The urge to see more overwhelmed him.

Elijah caught him staring. When Daniel looked back into his eyes, there was a mischievous twinkle there. They understood each other's intention perfectly.

"Hungry?" Elijah asked.

"Very," Daniel admitted. "But not for food."

Elijah's grin widened.

"Let's do something about that."

* * * *

Elijah's stateroom was the closest. As the door slammed

behind them, they were all over each other. Elijah shoved him against the wall, pushing his strong body against him.

Daniel wrapped his arms around Elijah's shoulders and drew him closer, feeling his strength. He moved his hand across the back of Elijah's neck and he thrust his fingers into the luxurious thickness of his hair. He wanted to experience all of him at once. His senses were overwhelmed by the touch of him, the heat and the taste.

Oh God. Have I ever been with a man as exciting as this? The answer was no.

Elijah pushed his tongue between his lips, filling his mouth, and ground his hips against Daniel's. The bulge of his cock was promisingly thick. They breathed hot and heavy into each other. Daniel couldn't wait.

He dragged Elijah impatiently toward the bed.

"Eager for something?" Elijah whispered.

"Desperate."

Daniel sat on the edge of the bed and tore at Elijah's fly. He was out of control. He never behaved like this. Elijah had brought out the animal in him. He relied entirely on instinct. Shoving Elijah's trousers to his knees, his eyes flashed briefly on the hairy thickness of his thighs before he snatched his white underpants and tore them down. There would be time to explore the finer details of his body later. Right now, his need was more urgent.

Elijah's cock did not disappoint him. Beautifully thick and long, it was as handsomely made as the rest of him. Daniel grabbed the shaft in one hand and cupped his heavy balls in the other. It was superb. He eased the foreskin back with his mouth then took it slow and deep, savoring its thickness, its heat, its sticky salty taste. His jaw ached pleasantly with the effort.

"Oh God," Elijah groaned, twisting his fingers softly around Daniel's head. "Take it easy. You've got me turned up high."

Daniel hollowed his cheeks, sucking on just the head, tasting the full flavor of it. He loved to hear the helpless catch in Elijah's breath. He had him right on the edge but wouldn't let him go over. Not yet. He gave his balls a gentle tug downward, judging by his reaction just how far to go, how much pressure to apply.

"Don't make me come," Elijah moaned. "I want to fuck you."

Daniel eased back. He wouldn't be fulfilled until Elijah fucked him too. Couldn't let him come too soon, however badly he wanted his load. Later — he would taste his fill. He squeezed his shaft, milking pre-cum to the tip, lapping it up before sitting back, his face flushed.

"Let's do it," he said urgently.

Hurriedly they undressed. Clothes flew across the room. Fingers grabbing cocks, nipples, buttocks. Daniel ran his hands across Elijah's chest, over his belly and around his waist, rapidly trying to experience all of him. He possessed all the attributes he found attractive in a man. All in one faultless, masculine package. He was a fantasy made flesh — hard, hairy, magnificent flesh.

Elijah took him in his arms, swung him around and held him facedown on the bed. Daniel shivered as Elijah softly pressed his lips against his shoulder. Gooseflesh prickled. His whole body responded to Elijah's touch. Elijah pressed a tender stream of kisses down the curve of his spine.

Daniel's body juddered.

"Feel good?" Elijah murmured, moving his lips across the skin.

"Oh God, yes."

"I'm just getting started."

He came to the small of Daniel's back. The caress of his lips was featherlight.

Daniel squirmed. This feeling, this anticipation was exquisite. But it was also torture. He wanted Elijah. Wanted him now. Elijah's breath blew hot along his butt crack. He spread his cheeks. Daniel let out a long, satisfied sigh as Elijah pushed his lips against his tender opening.

Oh God. He gripped the bedclothes. The sensation was

insanely pleasurable. Elijah knew exactly what to do with his tongue.

"Stop teasing," Daniel gasped at last. "Just fuck me. Fuck me *now!*"

Elijah gave his arse a soft tap and leapt from the bed, bounding to the bathroom. He came back moments later with a strip of condoms and a bottle of lube. Daniel smiled, glad they were on the same page and he didn't have to ask. Elijah ripped into the wrapper then covered his dick in rubber and palmed lube from head to base. He squeezed more lube onto his fingers and thrust them into the crack of Daniel's butt, finding the opening, easing the way.

Daniel squirmed.

"Everything okay?" Elijah asked. "I don't want to hurt you."

"You won't," Daniel said, pushing up onto his hands and knees. "Get inside me."

Elijah came up close behind. One hand on Daniel's hip, he steered his cock to his tight butt. Gently he nudged the opening, and pushed a little harder till the resistance gave way. Daniel wanted to cry, it felt so damn good, but instead he relaxed his body, willing Elijah to go farther. Gripping his waist with both hands, he eased all the way in.

They groaned when Elijah's hips pressed against his arse. This was it. They were tied together. Complete.

Time ceased to exist. Outside a strong wind howled around the ship and the heavy seas that had long been forecast began to roll. In Elijah's stateroom they were oblivious to all of it. The world had shrunk to the scope of the cabin.

Daniel was in heaven as Elijah moved him about the bed. Changing positions, so he lay on his back with Elijah on top of him. This was even more perfect, allowing them to look into each other's eyes while they made love. He folded his arms and legs around Elijah's back, locking him deep inside. Despite the grand portions of his cock, it seemed to fit Daniel perfectly. His body adjusted to the massive intrusion and there was no pain, only intense, unspoiled pleasure.

They came at the same time, eyes locked. Elijah erupted with his cock buried deep while Daniel splashed a white-hot mess against their hairy bellies.

They lay together, still connected, Daniel's limbs wrapped around Elijah's body, kissing. Still hungry for each other. Finally Elijah pulled his weight back and they came apart.

"I didn't hurt you, did I?"

"Not at all," Daniel said. "Quite the opposite. I don't know when I was last fucked like that. If ever." It was true. He couldn't recall feeling such sexual satisfaction.

Elijah chuckled, rising from the bed and removing the condom. Daniel watched him walk to the bathroom. What a sight. He had strong hamstrings and a meaty, nicely furred arse. There was a delicate patch of soft brown hair in the small of his back. On some guys that could be quite off-putting but on Elijah it was another piece of the jigsaw that made him so fucking hot.

Elijah returned from the bathroom. His soft cock swayed — still impressively sized.

"Hungry now?" he asked, flopping on the bed beside Daniel.

"Only for more of you," he said, rolling in for another kiss.

Chapter Ten

"You're in a faraway place," Anouska said.

"Sorry." Elijah realized he'd been staring into space for several minutes.

The afternoon with Daniel was all he could think about. He would still be in bed with him now if Daniel wasn't so committed to his show. He knew what it was like for a performer – the last thing needed before a big performance was distraction. But what a distraction it had been.

They were in Cafe24 for a light snack ahead of the show. Anouska had the evening off. She'd been entertaining a kids' party all afternoon and didn't have to work again until Saturday's finale. She told Elijah she wanted to check out Daniel's show before going to bed early.

"What's the matter?" she asked. "Is this a come-down after your success last night?"

"No. It's nothing." He shrugged, trying to keep it light. He wasn't ready to spill on what he'd been up to. Not so soon after Vladislav. Being with Daniel was one hundred percent different, one hundred percent better, but no one else would see that. They'd just see a big old tramp working his through the company cuties.

"It looks like something," Anouska said, tucking into a huge plate of pasta in cream sauce with lashings of cheese. With no show to prepare for, she was treating herself to a carb overload.

Elijah toyed with a small selection of cured meats and olives. His date with Daniel was still on and he didn't want to spoil his appetite. He planned to watch the first show, then shower and change in the interval before catching the second act. The set list would be the same for both, but he didn't care. He wouldn't miss the opportunity of seeing him live.

"You should hear some of the things being said about Daniel backstage," Anouska said, wiping her mouth with a napkin.

His eyes narrowed. "By who?"

"Oliver Gill. Apparently, Daniel and he used to know each other. A long time ago. Oliver can't stand him."

"Oliver is a vicious little shit." Elijah hardly knew him but he sounded like a prize dick. That cack-handed pass he'd made in the dressing room had not endeared him and now he bad-mouthing Daniel to anyone who'd listen. "They scarcely know each other. Oliver lost a couple of jobs to Daniel years ago and still holds a grudge. Whatever he says has been blown out of all proportion."

"I know that," Anouska said. "He's been a trumped-up diva from the minute he came on board. I don't think we'll be seeing much of him after the cruise. He's pissed off far too many people. I get the impression that Helen wants rid of him."

"I only met him yesterday but he seems wildly erratic."

"I feel a bit sorry for him," she admitted. "He's a troubled spirit. He can only cope by lashing out. Even when someone tries being nice to him, he fights it. It's instinct. Like animal survival."

"He needs help then," Elijah said.

"Sure, he does. But he'll never ask for it. I doubt he realizes that he does it."

They finished their food and headed to the theater. Despite talk of Oliver, Elijah was excited about everything. About what had happened that afternoon and what would come this evening. He could still smell Daniel's manly scent. It lingered on his skin. He remembered the heat and hardness of his body. He couldn't wait to hold him again. It wouldn't be long.

Elijah didn't want to distract Daniel from the show, so they sat halfway back in the center of the stalls. Close enough to see, without being seen. The house filled up quickly and by the time Helen came on stage to introduce him all the seats were taken.

Elijah felt a frisson of excitement. As exciting as performing himself, without the apprehension and stage fright of facing a crowd.

The applause was huge as the band struck up and Daniel strode on stage for his first song, an upbeat version of *Love Hurts*. Dressed in a sharp blue suit and open-necked shirt, he looked handsome, exceptionally so. He'd tidied his stubble since the afternoon. Elijah was glad he hadn't gone for a perfectly clean shave. The stubble suited him. Big time.

Elijah grinned all through the song. Daniel was a showman and gave everything to the number. At the end of the first song, he chatted to the audience and had them in the palm of his hand. Warm and funny, he name-checked a couple of people in the first row. He was a natural and made it look effortless. He sang a big ballad next, revealing the full range of his voice.

The audience showed their appreciation. Elijah could feel it. It came off them in waves. This was so much better than what they were used to. Daniel Blake was in a league of his own.

He brought the pace up with a medley of songs from *Jersey Boys*, moving and dancing about the stage, getting the audience to clap along. Elijah forgot about their personal relationship and watched him as a fan. He *was* a fan. At the end, he got to his feet with the rest of them, shouting for more.

Daniel obliged with his encore before thanking them for being such a great crowd and disappearing into the wings.

"Oh my God," Anouska raved. "Oliver is full of shit. *That* was incredible. What a voice."

"Exceptional."

"And damn fine to look at too."

Elijah left the theater on a high. What a sensational start to the night. And it could only get better. Soon, very soon, he would spend some quality time with the star of the evening.

And he couldn't wait.

* * * *

The reception was something else. Better than anything Daniel had expected. Maybe because it was the penultimate evening, the passengers were so much more responsive. By the end of the second show the entire theater were on their feet. Another standing ovation.

Overwhelming. What a show. What a night.

He had no time to hang about. As Helen came on stage to close the show and let the passengers know what to expect tomorrow — on their final day — Daniel rushed through the wings and along the crew corridor that took him to the main foyer of the theater. A long table had been set, displaying both of his albums on CD. Daniel positioned himself behind the table with a young member of the crew just as the doors opened and the audience spilled out.

The next twenty minutes were insane as he signed CDs and posed for photographs. It gave him a brief snapshot of what life must be like for the super famous, on the scale of Beyoncé or Justin Bieber.

With a dozen or so people left in line, the stock of CDs ran out. "That's it," the attendant told him. "Everything gone."

He apologized to the remaining guests and posed for photos with those who wanted them.

This part of the job never got old — putting a smile on people's faces. He didn't want anyone who attended his shows to leave thinking it was just okay or good enough, he wanted them to go with a huge smile, having had a wonderful time. That alone made it worth the effort he put in.

When the last guest left the foyer, he made his way to the dressing room. The night had been a success, no doubt about it. Two massive shows and a sell out on his albums.

His whole body buzzed as he walked through the empty stalls.

And it was far from over. If anything, the best was still to come.

In the privacy of his room, he stripped to his underpants and hurriedly washed his face and torso in the small sink. Ideally, he'd like a shower but that would delay him further. The meet-and-greet session had lasted longer than expected. Right now, his only aim was to freshen up and meet Elijah as quickly as possible.

He dried swiftly then sprayed his arm pits with deodorant and gave his upper body a spritz of Invictus cologne. He put on blue jeans, a white shirt and a blue checked jacket. The ship rolled from side to side as he fixed his hair in the mirror. At last he was good to go. Eleven-thirty. Half an hour later than planned.

They'd arranged to meet in Vintages wine bar on Deck Five. With dim lights, oversized furnishings and as extensive wine list, it was the ideal place to unwind. The music played low and at this time of night it was usually quiet, with guests favoring the more upbeat bars, featuring live music and DJs.

Elijah waited at the bar, chatting to one of the waiters. He wore an open-necked shirt and dark jacket. Casually smart. Totally handsome.

"I hope you didn't think I'd stood you up," Daniel said, moving close to him. He smelled as good as he looked.

"Are you kidding? I'm just glad to see you at all. I saw the size of the crowd waiting to meet you. I didn't think you'd get away before midnight."

"Crazy, wasn't it?"

"You earned it and you deserved it. I saw you on that stage. You had the crowd in the palm of your hand. They loved you."

"Well, that part is over, now it's just us. No audience. That'll do me for the rest of the night."

Their eyes met, maintaining the contact. Everything

Daniel had experienced till then was forgotten. The entire world fell away, like a curtain with just the two of them still on stage.

"Want to order some wine?" Elijah asked. "Or are you hungry? Would you rather go for food first?"

"No, I need a drink. Food can wait."

"That's what I hoped you'd say."

Elijah called for a bottle of Malbec. The waiter told them to find a seat and he would bring the wine over. They chose a quiet table in the corner with two comfortable red leather chairs, a glass-topped coffee table and a Tiffany-style lamp.

Daniel sank into the comforting depths of the chair. "It's good to sit down at last. I don't know about you, but when I'm on stage the effect of the ship's movement seems magnified. I feel like I spent most of the show tensing my legs to keep from falling over."

"The old girl is rolling about a bit tonight," Elijah said. "I took a peak outside earlier and the sea is definitely picking up. But I get what you're saying. The effect is more pronounced from the stage. Nobody would know though. You're singing was flawless."

"I'm glad it came across that way."

Their wine arrived. The waiter poured and left them alone. Daniel gave his glass a few turns to unlock the flavor. He took a deep sniff before tasting.

"Wow," he said. "Great choice."

"Do you know a lot about wine?"

"No so much. My dad was a great wine drinker. He liked to go on courses and when he opened a bottle at the dinner table, he would tell us all about it first. Make us smell it before drinking, check out the color and the legs. He wasn't a snob about it, nothing like that, but he liked a glass of something decent."

"Doesn't everyone?"

"I certainly do. Cheers." They clinked glasses.

"Cheers. Are you close to your parents?" Elijah asked.

"Very close, though my dad passed away a few years

ago."

"Oh, I'm sorry. You did mention that before."

"It's all right now." The hurt over losing his father remained but the pain was different now. No longer as crippling. "He's the reason I'm here. I was working at sea when he took ill and I cut short my contract. I've always felt like I have unfinished business because of that. That's why I came back. To see out a season and put that business to bed."

Elijah's eyes were wide and dark. "Did it work?"

"It feels that way. I'm ready to move on to something new when I get home."

"And what will that be? After your stint in panto."

Daniel laughed. "Who knows? I'll take stock over the winter, assess my options and see what next year brings." He was confident about the future, despite having no jobs lined up beyond the panto season. His manager was task master and Daniel had inherited a strong work ethic from his parents. He would take whatever opportunity came his way.

They worked their way through the bottle of Malbec. Elijah was fine company. Smart, witty, funny, sexy — a lethal combination. Daniel couldn't stop looking at him. At his eyes, his mouth, his hair, his hands — every part irresistible. He remembered that afternoon and how those hands had felt on his body. How perfectly compatible they were.

"You know one of the things I love most?" Elijah said. "This." He gestured to the near-empty bar. "Peace and quiet. There's nothing like it. The space to have a conversation, or to think, or read. I appreciate the roar of an audience like any performer, but there's nothing like escaping from the crowd. Do you know what I'm saying?"

"Completely," Daniel said. "Mellow weekends. Lazy Sundays with a pot of coffee, the newspapers or a good book."

"Now you're talking my language. Papers in the morning, a roast lunch and a nice long book in the afternoon. Someone

to share the quiet with. I couldn't ask for more than that."
Elijah had a wide, irresistible grin on his face. "Think you
could go for that?"

Daniel's balls tightened. "As long as reading isn't the only
thing you want to do with your Sundays."

Elijah leaned closer. "If I was with you, the damn papers
wouldn't get a look."

Daniel was hot. The tension in his nuts spread all the way
up through his belly into his chest. It sat heavily in the air
between them. One spark would set the room alight. He'd
never wanted anything as badly as he did right now.

The bottle of wine was empty. They gazed longingly
across the table.

"Are you hungry yet?" Elijah asked. "Want to find
something to eat?"

He hadn't eaten in six hours but food was the last thing
he wanted. "The only place still serving is Cafe24. Not the
most romantic venue I can think of."

Elijah's soulful brown eyes considered his. "I've got a
better idea. How does room service sound?"

"Just the thing. Your place or mine this time?"

* * * *

They stood under the shower in Elijah's bathroom. As the
deck swayed in the swell, they were steady against each
other. Daniel explored Elijah's body as though feeling him
for the first time. It had only been a few hours since they'd
been naked together… This was something new. While
they were locked together at the mouth, Daniel caressed
the broad sweep of Elijah's shoulders, the long curve of this
spine, the extraordinary fullness of his arse. Every part of
him was perfect.

Daniel's heart beat wildly. He'd never been this intimate
with another man so quickly. He'd had one-night stands
before — not many guys his age hadn't — and slept with men
on the first date. They were no big deal. This was different.

Showering together, discovering each other's bodies, keeping nothing back. *This definitely is a big deal.*

And it had happened so quickly. After two heavy shows, he wanted to get clean before getting it on. He felt way too funky after his time on stage. He suggested Elijah pour them a couple of drinks from the mini bar while he cleaned up, but in no time at all, they were naked and kissing inside the tiny stall.

The kisses didn't stop. Openmouthed, they yielded to each other with a fiery passion. Daniel knew his lips would be raw in the morning if they kept this up. He didn't care. All that mattered was the man in his arms.

And this arse. Daniel couldn't leave it alone. He dug his fingers into the meaty flesh and mashed the cheeks together. *It is awesome.*

Their wet, soapy bodies pressed tight in the narrow stall. These showers were never designed to hold two people, but they managed, squeezing in. When they needed each other as powerfully as this, they would always find a way. They ground their slippery torsos together and their cocks slid against each other in the tightness between. The sensations were exquisite. Almost too much.

Daniel broke free of Elijah's kiss and moved his lips along the firm line of his jaw, brushed the softness of his stubble, progressing across his neck. Elijah shuddered and tipped back his head as Daniel drew his tongue along the sensitive skin.

"Man, that's intense," Elijah sighed, raking his fingers through Daniel's wet hair.

The ship gave a sudden lurch and they fell against the tiled wall, laughing.

"No, *this* is intense," Daniel said, grabbing Elijah's arse again, kneading the soapy cheeks with both hands.

Elijah moaned, pressing the side of his face against Daniel's. "Is that what you want?"

"You know it is."

Daniel drew his cheeks apart and moved his fingers into

the crevice. He found the searing hot opening and gently tested it with the tip of his finger. Elijah wrapped his arms around Daniel's shoulders and rose onto his toes, offering full access. Daniel entered him easily. With the hot water, the excitement of being together, Elijah was totally relaxed and ready to receive him. He pushed in deeper. Elijah's arse gripped him, hot and tight.

That afternoon, Daniel had bottomed for Elijah. It was what they both wanted at the time. Now they wanted something different. Daniel had always been versatile and instinct told him Elijah was too.

His instincts were one hundred percent right.

He wriggled another finger inside and slid them back and forth. Elijah gripped his shoulders tighter.

"Enough," he growled. "Just fuck me now."

Daniel smiled. Damn good to hear him say it and catch the note of begging in his voice.

He shut off the water and they hopped quickly from the shower. As they hastily toweled themselves down, their hard cocks bounced. Daniel couldn't keep his eyes off Elijah's beautiful brown-skinned dick. The way the delicate pink head protruded slightly from the folds of foreskin. He pulled Elijah in for another openmouthed kiss.

"I want you now," he said passionately.

"Let's do it."

They hurried into the bedroom. Still damp, Elijah leapt on the bed, getting up on all fours while Daniel grabbed a strip of condoms and a bottle of lube. As he primed his dick, he took in the glorious sight Elijah presented — knees spread, big arse raised and open, balls hanging heavily between his thighs. A feast for his eyes.

Daniel got on the bed behind him and prepared his hole with a couple of well-lubed fingers, pushing the cool gel deep into the passage. His arse was tight but accommodating. Daniel still asked, "Everything okay?"

"Perfect," Elijah moaned, setting his stance. "Now give it to me."

All his senses were heightened as Daniel got into position behind him, nowhere more than the head of his cock. He rubbed it up and down the lightly furred crack before moving in on the opening. One hand on Elijah's hip, the other at the base of his dick, he entered, pushing smoothly to the hilt. All the way in, he held Elijah's waist in both hands, keeping his arse pressed tight against his hips.

He breathed deeply, savoring the contact, the feeling of completion. The bed moved with the ocean but they remained together.

"I love it," Elijah said, lifting his arse higher, changing the angle.

Daniel groaned, pressing into him.

They made love with passion and hunger. Daniel had waited a long time to feel this kind of connection with a man. Sex was always good, but never like this. Pushing forward, easing back, but never withdrawing completely. He didn't want to break the connection. They rolled like the ocean within each other.

Elijah rose onto his knees. Daniel wrapped his arms around his chest, pulling their upper bodies tight, still fucking. Elijah turned his head, mouth open, tongue thrust forward. Daniel leaned over, making contact to complete the kiss. He dropped his hands to Elijah's cock, feeling its hardness, its wetness. He took the head in his palm, rubbing gently.

"Close to coming," Elijah said.

"Let's do it together."

Daniel moved his hips faster. He'd been holding back. Listening to Elijah's breathing, judging the tension in his body and cock, he timed it perfectly, taking them to the edge and over at the same time. Elijah's arse tightened around him as they came, dragging out the climax.

It seemed to be endless.

They fell forward, still joined, sweating and gasping. Elijah was hot and slippery beneath him. Eventually Daniel withdrew and went to the bathroom to get rid of the condom.

When he returned, Elijah lay on his back, propped up on pillows. His legs were wide, presenting the lovely sight of his still semi-hard cock.

"I'm hungry now, aren't you?"

Now that he thought about it, Daniel realized he was starving. It had been some night—two shows, awesome sex—and he'd burned a lot of energy. He'd have to replenish it before going again.

Elijah ordered burgers and fries from room service.

Dressed in white robes, they tackled the mini bar before the food arrived, taking a vodka each and sharing a Diet Coke mixer.

"I can't believe this has happened," Elijah said as they sat on the leather sofa, angled to look at each other. "I mean, meeting someone like you, just as we're going home."

Daniel stroked the back of his hand. "Unreal, isn't it? Though it wouldn't have been much better if we met earlier in the summer. We would still set off in different directions after a few days. We're travelers."

"I'd have changed my itinerary to be near to you."

Daniel smiled at his honesty. Elijah could admit that his feelings were as strong as his own.

"I'd like to see you again," Daniel said. "When we leave the ship. I know we only met yesterday but I don't want it to end. Not yet."

Elijah squeezed his hand tenderly. His dark eyes glittered in the soft light. "It won't. You live in Leeds, right? I'm heading to Salford. It's not like we're going to opposite ends of the country. What is that? Forty miles maximum. An hour's drive in really bad traffic."

Daniel hadn't thought of that. An hour was nothing. So what if the cruise was almost over? They could still see each other. Every day if they wanted to—with minimal effort. People traveled farther to get to work.

Suddenly they were across the sofa and in each other's arms again. Kissing. He slid his hand inside Elijah's robe, trailing his fingers through his chest hair. Locating his nipples, he gently pinched and elongated the tip. He reached lower. Elijah was hard again, his big dick rising through the front of his robe.

They were cut short by a knock at the door.

Elijah groaned. "Who's ever heard of punctual room service? That stuff usually takes hours."

"Maybe it's just as well," Daniel chuckled. "You wore me out first time. I need to eat before we go again."

The burgers, washed down with vodka and Coke, were delicious. Daniel devoured his plate in minutes.

"Whoa, you certainly were hungry," Elijah said, sweeping his uneaten fries onto Daniel's plate.

"I didn't realize it myself."

"Eat up, sexy boy. I don't want you going weak on me."

They made love again. With their hunger and the urgency of their earlier passion satiated, they took their time, delving into each other with eyes, hands and mouths. Nowhere off limit. When Elijah put on a condom and drove his cock into Daniel's butt, their union was accomplished in full. They gave and accepted every part of themselves.

Beyond their balcony, the Atlantic Ocean was in turmoil as a storm mounted, but it paled in significance compared to the burgeoning force of their developing love.

Chapter Eleven

By Saturday morning, the ship was at the mercy of the ocean and its elements. Neither its size nor the state-of-the-art stabilizers could prevent the enormous vessel from pitching in fifteen-foot waves. There were considerably fewer people on the decks and breakfast in Cafe24 was the quietest it had been in weeks.

Though a large proportion of the passengers suffered the queasy effects of high seas in the Atlantic, for the crew members this was just another day. The *Anthem* had been built to sustain far worse. Some motion was to be expected. They were at sea after all. No matter how large a vessel was, the ocean was always bigger.

Anouska Frost had experienced worse seas than this. Two years ago, while dancing on a Royal Caribbean ship, they'd encountered a hurricane en route from Florida to the Bahamas. Passengers had been confined to their staterooms for twelve long hours while the captain had tried to hold the ship steady in forty-foot waves. After that particular voyage, Anouska could take anything the ocean threw at her.

Including Terry St. King.

At eight-thirty on Saturday morning they stood on the main stage of the theater trying to get Terry up to speed with the routine Helen expected him to perform in the finale that evening. A detailed technical rehearsal with the band, dancers, singers and guest artists was scheduled for eleven but Terry wanted extra practice before then.

Anouska was tasked with putting together the routine for *Copacabana*. Simple enough. The group had performed this song so many times they could do it without thinking. It was second nature. But Terry wasn't part of the group. He usually sat at his piano and walked out center stage to take a bow. Full stage production numbers were a thing of the very distant past.

"Terry, why don't you stand somewhere near the front of the stage and we'll dance around you. Concentrate on the singing and let us worry about the movement." She had already simplified the routine twice since he had come to her yesterday asking for extra help.

"No," he said indignantly. "They're expecting a show and I mean to give them a show. I can't just stand there like a bloody plank, darling. Helen would love that. She's searching for an excuse to get rid of me and I won't give her the satisfaction. My audience have been denied my headline act, so I will damn well dazzle them with this bloody awful song. Walk me through it again."

Terry was already unsteady on his feet as the stage pitched and rolled beneath them. If the weather didn't improve, they would have to perform a vastly simplified version of the choreography. But Anouska humored him and ran through the number again.

She felt sorry for the old boy. Most people hated him, with good reason. He could be an outright shit without even trying, belittling other performers and their ability. But it was an act. Despite years of experience he was a deeply insecure person. Whatever talent he used to possess had long gone. His voice was shot. Terry knew it as well as everyone else. He had no choice but to hide behind the persona of a bitchy old queen — the grand dame of the seas.

Even today he dressed the part, rocking up for rehearsal in drainpipe white trousers, a lilac shirt, a white waistcoat and white trilby. His glittery shoes boasted a Cuban heel while his fingers and wrists sparkled with more garish jewelry than a Soho drag queen.

"I think you're getting it," Anouska said as he completed another walk through of the routine.

"Do you think so?" he asked, his eyes bright and hopeful. For a moment, the mask had slipped.

"Absolutely," she enthused. "That was superb. And don't forget, tonight we'll have a full house. You always produce that spark of star quality when you've got an audience to play to." Outrageous flattery, but he needed it. She hated to see anyone so down.

"That's very true," Terry said. "The audience is oxygen to a performer like myself. Without it, we're nothing. Let's give it one more try."

Anouska was starving. She had skipped breakfast to meet Terry at seven-thirty. But if it took one more run to instill the confidence he needed to walk out here later that was fine. She suspected a lot of his anxiety was down to Daniel. The younger man with an amazing voice. intimidated Terry. Quite unnecessarily.

Daniel was a lovely guy and Elijah adored him. From what she'd seen of him, she doubted he'd intentionally do anything to make Terry feel uncomfortable. Not intentionally. She'd met plenty of egomaniacs who got off on putting people down. Daniel wasn't that type. Anouska had always possessed a good bullshit detector. She could spot an arsehole at fifty paces, and Daniel wasn't one.

He'd probably be mortified if he knew how anxious he made Terry.

But there were few things more fragile or irrational than a showbiz ego. Terry's insecurity might be misplaced but Anouska knew nothing she said in relation to Daniel would change it. Terry's mind was made up.

"I think that will do for now," he said at the end of the number. "As you say, there's only so much more I can add without the magic of an audience."

"You'll knock 'em dead," she said. "I promise."

"You're too kind. Thank you for doing this. I wouldn't ask just anyone."

"It's been a pleasure."

"Yes, it has, hasn't it? So I'll see you back here at eleven.

Ta-ta for now." With a regal wave, Terry left the stage.

Anouska smiled. He really wasn't so bad. People would realize that if he wasn't so arch with them. Even Helen would come around if he gave her a chance and wasn't at her throat the whole time.

She drew on her hoodie and headed backstage. There was no one else around. They'd been practicing without musical accompaniment, just counting steps. Much easier that way, when trying to teach someone a new routine. Hopefully he'd remember the count and not get too distracted when they ran it with the live band.

This time tomorrow it would all be over. Though Anouska would be staying on board for the first three months of the North American season, a lot of the crew were leaving. It wouldn't be the same when most of her fellow Brits left the *Anthem* in Southampton to be succeeded by American entertainers. It was her choice to stay but she'd miss her colleagues terribly. Though the parent company, Royal Atlantic, liked to match their itinerary with local entertainers, they preferred not to have a complete change of staff at the beginning of each new season. There was a period of bedding in with the new crew when experienced old hands were appreciated.

Besides, she would get to spend Christmas in the Caribbean this year. Now *that* was something to look forward to. *This job certainly has its perks.*

Walking through the darkened wings, she suddenly became conscious of movement ahead of her. Expecting one of the technicians to step into view, she quickly realized that something wasn't right. Whoever it was proceeded in a furtive, stealthy, clearly not wanting to bring attention to themselves. Anouska took a silent step into the shadows and waited.

It must be a passenger. It wasn't unheard of for curious guests to explore the ship on their own, gaining entry to the crew areas. Earlier in the year a sommelier from the main restaurant had been fired after getting caught with two

American tourists in his cabin. He had flirted with them for the duration of their voyage and on the second-to-last night they'd determined to pay him a visit, making their way through two decks that were off limits to passengers. By allowing them in, he'd sealed their fate. He'd lost his job and the ladies had been blacklisted from future Royal Atlantic cruises.

No doubt this was someone with a similar intention. On the last day at sea they chose to take a sneaky look around. *Well, not on my watch.* She wouldn't get anyone in trouble by calling security. When they finally showed themselves, she'd send them back to the passenger quarters. No harm done.

Up ahead, a figure in the shadows stuck close to the wall. Moving slowly, they approached the dressing room reserved for headline acts, opened the door and slipped inside.

Someone did not want to be seen. *Someone up to no good.*

But going into a private dressing room — that was taking it too far.

Anouska strode toward the door and shoved it open. She had surprise on her side. "This is a private area," she said staunchly. "What are you doing here?"

Oliver Gill stood beside the dressing table, startled by the sight of her.

"Anouska," he hissed. "What the fuck?"

"Oliver." She was equally surprised.

He looked hideous. He never had the healthiest appearance, even on a good day, but right now he looked like hell. His eyes were sunken within heavily shadowed pits. His skin had the pallor of a washed-out tea towel. The dumbstruck expression on his face told of only one thing — guilt.

"What are you doing creeping around here?" she asked.

"I'm not creeping around," he snapped defensively. "You're the one who barged in like a fucking lunatic."

"Oliver, I saw you come in here. You were hiding. What

the hell are you up to?"

"Nothing." He stood with one hand behind his back.

"What have you got there?"

"It's nothing. Now fuck off."

Looking at him, ridden with guilt, she remembered the entertainment schedule for that afternoon. Daniel had a matinee at two o'clock.

Of course.

Oliver had spent the last two days slagging Daniel off to anyone who would listen. Much like Terry, Daniel's talent and success intimidated Oliver. It was no secret that he hated him.

"You're trying to sabotage the show," she said accusingly.

Oliver looked fleetingly at her, then beyond, to the door. She stood between him and the exit.

"What show? What the hell are you talking about? You've lost it, you mad bitch."

Anouska stood firm. "If you won't tell me, how about we get Helen and Orestis in here? You can tell *them* what you're doing."

"For fuck's sake." He smiled, exasperated. "You're such a drama queen. I'm not doing anything, okay. I'm looking for my phone, that's all. I came in here the other night to see Elijah. I thought I might have left it. I just came to check."

"Elijah told me all about your visit," Anouska said. The phone story was bullshit. He wasn't a good enough liar to make her believe him. "He said you were off your face."

"No I wasn't. Why would he say that?"

"Whatever," she said. "What have you got behind your back?"

"I've already told you. Are you fucking deaf? It's none of your business."

"This is the last day — a big day — I'm not having you wreck it for everyone else. Just because you're jealous. You're pathetic. Whatever it is you're planning, it's *not* happening. Understand?"

She strode angrily toward him. This had gone far enough.

Oliver moved away, angling his body to keep the object behind his back concealed. Undeterred, Anouska grabbed one of his arms. She was fitter than him, stronger, and dragged it out from behind.

Oliver held a small, three-hundred milliliter bottle of water. Anouska wasn't stupid. She'd seen plenty of backstage pranks during her career. She'd been the victim of them herself. She seized the bottle from his hand.

"All right, what's in here?" Looking at the bottle, she saw the seal was broken. Laxative was her best guess. An old favorite of pranksters everywhere.

"Give me that back." Oliver grabbed for the bottle but she held it easily out of reach.

"Not till you tell me what it is."

"It's water. Just water."

He reached again, but she gracefully stepped out of his way. His reaction, the furious look on his face, was proof of the lie. Whatever was in the bottle, he didn't want her to find out.

"This is going straight to Helen. You can tell her what you proposed to do with it."

Oliver came at her with a speed she didn't foresee. Head down, he rammed into her stomach. His arms went around her waist and he took her to the floor in a rugby tackle. Stunned and winded, Anouska's reactions were slow, too slow. Oliver pushed his advantage, laying his weight on her torso.

"Give me that fucking bottle," he spat in her face.

Anouska struggled to breathe. What was he doing? The weight on her chest, it was too much, crushing her. One look at his face and she knew she had totally underestimated him. His eyes were ablaze with fury. His features contorted in an ugly mask of hate.

"Oliver," she gasped. "Please."

His breath, sour with last night's alcohol, was hot against her face.

"*Please*," he mimicked. "Please what, you interfering

bitch?"

Fear gripped her. That look in his eyes — he was capable of anything. The weight on her chest got heavier, crushing her ribs. He thrust his forearms against her throat, squeezing on her windpipe.

He's going to kill me. She knew it with terrifying certainty. *Oh my God. This is real.*

"Stop." She tried to speak. The sound was a strangled croak.

"It's your own fault," he said. His sneering face was right on top of her. "Smug, interfering cunt. You're as bad as all of them. Think you're so much better than me. No. Fucking. Way."

The pressure of his arm against her throat increased, crushing her windpipe.

There was an explosion of stars before Anouska's vision clouded and her world slipped into darkness.

Dead. She was dead.

Extraordinary. He felt it. He literally felt it. The moment her spirit, life force, whatever the hell it was — he felt it as it left her body. One second it was Anouska lying under him, the next just a lifeless thing.

He had done that. Just him. Nobody else.

He'd killed her.

Easing his weight from her corpse, he sat on the floor, staring at her for the longest time. Not knowing what to think. Unsure of how he felt.

The floor rolled from side to side beneath him. He had killed someone, but the ship kept moving, the ocean kept churning. The world did not end.

Only time seemed unreal. Dreamlike.

He didn't know how long he sat there for. Ten minutes? Fifteen?

Slowly he came back into himself. The state of shock subsided.

One thought was more terrifying than the fact he

murdered Anouska Frost—he had enjoyed it. He *liked* it. The taste of power, of his own importance. He felt it when staring at her body and it frightened him. He'd taken a life and it was the most wonderful feeling.

Now what?

Self-preservation, that's what.

No way was he going to pay for this.

Why should I? She was nobody. Just a third-rate dancer in the chorus of a shitty ship's company. She deserved what she got. She practically asked for it, snooping around, sticking her nose into business that had nothing to do with her. What was the stupid bitch doing down here anyway? At this time of day, the theater should be deserted.

Oliver's plan had been so simple. It was perfect—foolproof. It had come to him that morning as he woke up, fully formed. The GHB he'd scored from the sleazy couple in Lisbon. He would pour all he had left in a bottle of water and leave it in Daniel's dressing room. It was a hell of a dose. If Daniel wasn't used to the drug, it would render him unconscious. It might even tip him into a coma. Even if he was a seasoned druggie, which Oliver doubted—he was too boring for that—it would have a devastating effect and knock him senseless. Either way, Daniel wouldn't be singing today.

It had been a great plan. Ingenious in its simplicity. Until Anouska had come along and ruined it.

Interfering cunt.

Now she'd given him another problem. How to get rid of her body?

She would have to go over the side. That much was evident. In seas as rough as they were today, she would never be seen again. She'd be fish food. But he couldn't throw her in just yet. Not in daylight. He'd have to hide the body until it got dark.

Think, Oliver, think. It shouldn't be too difficult on a ship this size. There were plenty of places to conceal a corpse. Somewhere he could get at later without drawing attention to himself. How hard could it be?

A large suitcase. That would do it. Preferably one on wheels. No one would look twice if they saw him lugging a case around. Not on the last night of the cruise. There would be cases everywhere.

He would have to be quick. He had about an hour and half until the company would start to turn up for the rehearsal. His own suitcase would have to do for now. It was big enough. He could fit Anouska inside then stash it out of sight till later.

If he could get into a guest's stateroom, one with a balcony, while they were at dinner this evening, then he could chuck her into the ocean and no one would ever know. It was another perfect plan.

It was a shame, killing Anouska. If he'd intended to commit murder in the first place, he would have chosen Daniel. Gotten rid of him for good.

Still, one thing at a time.

The problem of Daniel Blake would keep for later.

Chapter Twelve

Elijah stretched and rolled against the heavenly body that lay beside him, pressing his hardness against Daniel's back. Daniel murmured appreciatively and leaned into Elijah's chest.

"This is nice," Daniel said, nudging his naked butt against Elijah's cock.

"It sure is," Elijah said, sliding an arm around Daniel's waist. He laid his hand flat against Daniel's belly and held him close, inhaling his sleepy smell. It felt like they had been at it all night with the energy of horny teenagers, dozing gently before one of them would rouse the other to do it again. He couldn't keep his hands off Daniel, wanting to hold him, touch him, kiss him, be inside him all the time. Thankfully Daniel's passion matched his own.

Despite his lack of sleep, Elijah felt fresher than an early spring morning.

The bed rolled from side to side as the ship plowed through heavy sea. The balcony creaked and groaned with the motion.

"Sounds like a real storm is brewing," Daniel said.

"I'll keep you safe," he replied, pressing a kiss into the small of Daniel's neck. "It's exciting, don't you think? Tossing around on the high seas."

"Maybe for you," Daniel laughed. "*You* don't have to do a show this afternoon."

"I'll hold your sick bag," he teased. "I'll be right there at the side of the stage. When you feel like puking, just let it rip."

"Wow, that's romance. Holding a sick bag."

"Yep," Elijah said. "I'm that kind of guy."

Daniel turned onto his back with open limbs. Elijah moved on top of him, taking his head in both hands and kissing with passion. Their cocks were hard, squeezed between their bodies. He couldn't get enough of Daniel, grinding against him, wanting to experience every inch of him, skin against skin.

This couldn't be more different from the other morning when he'd woken up next to Vladislav. He'd regretted that straight away. Even more so now. If he had known he was about to meet and fall in instant, crazy love, he would not have gone near Vladislav.

Too late now. He hadn't known Daniel then. Most people would do things differently if they saw what their future held. He couldn't change it—he could only move forward.

Daniel reached toward the dresser, grabbing condoms and lube. "Let me have you again," he growled.

"Are you sure?" Elijah said. They had fucked a hell of a lot last night. "Aren't you sore?"

Daniel spread his legs. "A little. But I still want you. Go easy on me."

Elijah happily obliged. He wrapped his arms around Daniel's body and entered him with the greatest care, easing his dick inside. With a lot of lube, deep breaths and kisses, their bodies became a single unit once more. They made love long and slow, sometimes barely stirring. Holding each other, looking in each other's eyes. Sharing.

They timed it perfectly, arriving together at a sweaty, shattering climax.

"Want to grab a quick breakfast before heading to the theater?" Elijah asked.

Daniel glanced at his watch. "I need to get back to my room first. A quick shower, a change of clothes. I don't think this just fucked, rolled-out-of-bed look will go down well around the ship."

"It suits you," Elijah said. "I could sure get used to seeing you like that."

"It might alarm the passengers."

"They'll all be sea sick today. They won't care."

As Daniel got up, Elijah made a grab for his sexy arse. "Don't take it away from me."

Daniel slipped away from him. "You can have it later. It needs a rest first."

Elijah lay back, watching while Daniel went through the room for his clothes. They'd been in such a hurry last night that their things were scattered everywhere. Still, it was a joy to watch his fine body move about the cabin, pulling on underwear, trousers, shirt and finally his shoes.

Elijah jumped from the bed, still naked, and took Daniel in his arms. "A kiss before you go."

"I'll only be twenty minutes."

"In that case, I'll need two kisses," he said, locking lips with Daniel.

When he left, Elijah couldn't stop smiling. It was unbelievable what a few hours with a gorgeous, sexy, intelligent and funny man could do. He couldn't remember when he'd last felt so carefree. Ever.

He turned on his iPod and brought up an old Elton John album, *Honkey Chateau*. He sang along at the top of his voice to *Mellow* while he showered. That was exactly how he felt — mellow. He soaped up his body with some reluctance, washing Daniel's scent off his skin. He wanted to keep the smell on him all day. If they weren't meeting in such a short time, that was exactly what he would have done.

The ship took an abrupt pitch to the right before jerking upright. Elijah steadied himself on the sink while he toweled off. They would have to take it easy on stage if these waves kept up.

He put on an old blue T-shirt with a portrait of Roger Moore as James Bond on the front, and a pair of red shorts. However cold it got at sea, it was always warm inside the ship, more so when rehearsing. He'd have time to change into something smarter ahead of Daniel's matinee.

Daniel was waiting in the foyer of Deck Five when Elijah

took the stairs up to meet him. He posed for photographs with a group of excited fans. Elijah stood back, watching as they went through the routine of passing cameras and phones around, changing position to stand next to him. Daniel took it with good grace. He was used to being recognized. Having been on TV himself, Elijah had had a small taste of fame, but nothing to the national recognition Daniel had gained. It was fun to watch the interplay he had with them. He had made time for everyone.

And he was beautiful. Elijah could watch him all day and never get bored.

Daniel had showered and washed his hair since he'd seen him last, but hadn't shaved. He'd opted for casual dress too. A white polo shirt with knee-length navy shorts and deck shoes. The shorts showed off his chunky calves, which only made Elijah horny again.

What had Daniel done to him? He had the sexual appetites of a rampant teen.

When Daniel finished with the last of his fans, Elijah stepped in before another could claim him and guided him into the coffee shop. He was ravenous.

"We'd better get these to go," Daniel said as they stepped up to the counter. "Rehearsal starts in ten minutes."

"But I'm starving," Elijah moaned.

"Me too. But that's what happens when you stay too late in bed."

"I wish we were still there."

"So do I."

They ordered coffee. A skinny latte for Elijah and a cappuccino for Daniel. Buttery croissants with ham and melted cheese and a giant triple chocolate chip cookie. Total indulgence but they deserved it.

The ship was in a deep sway. Passengers tottered from side to side as they tried to negotiate the central promenade. Some giggled with uneasy excitement, others looked worried while several were green and nauseous. Elijah was lucky. He'd never been a nervous traveler or suffered the ill effects of sea sickness. He smiled kindly at those who did. There was nothing worse than getting sick, especially when on holiday and trying to have a good time. The trick was to stay in the lower levels mid-ship where he were less likely to feel the violent motion.

The movement was more noticeable when they reached the theater in the bow. Every roll of the ship was accentuated. Neither of them was affected. They sat at the front of the stage with their legs hanging over the edge and attacked their breakfast with relish.

"Should have got more of these," Daniel said, swallowing the last mouthful of his ham-and-cheese croissant. "They're delicious."

Elijah agreed, pleased to see Daniel enjoying the food as much as he did. They matched each other in their appetites for just about everything. When all of this was over, he couldn't wait to cook for Daniel. Maybe next weekend, if they were both free, though they hadn't planned that far ahead. Elijah would have to get rid of his brother for the night. Harry had been crashing at his place since splitting with his wife. It was an ideal arrangement over the summer while Elijah worked away so much. He would never kick Harry out, he'd had a lousy year so far, but they would have to come to some kind of agreement that would give them both a bit of space within the flat. Especially if he wanted to give Daniel a permanent place in his life.

The band and the dancers filled the stage behind them. Elijah gathered all the empty wrappers together, binned them and they joined the rest of the group.

Helen and Orestis arrived and called the group to order. Despite the time, Helen was dressed to the nines in a tight red skirt, black top, white jacket and massive heels. Her hair had been blown dry and set in a white-blonde helmet. Elijah could smell her perfume from across the stage.

"Morning, everyone," she roared. "Last day for many of us. Are we going to have a good one? Yes?"

"Yes," the group cheered. Despite the lurching ship, the

atmosphere among the crew was jovial. It was like the last day of school.

"Everyone here?" Helen asked. "Are we ready to start?"

"We're still waiting for Anouska," one of the dancers answered.

Elijah looked around the stage and realized for the first time that his friend was missing. It was unlike her to be late. Her sense of punctuality was often exasperating.

"Anyone seen her?" Helen asked. "Tammy, you room together, don't you?"

Tammy, a young backing singer from Dorset, shook her head. "She went out early this morning. Before I woke up."

"She was with me," Terry St. King answered grandly. "In here. We had an early run through of my song."

Helen looked surprised. "You did? Did she say anything? Did she feel sick?"

"No. She was fine. She said she'd see me back here for this rehearsal thing."

"It's not like Anouska to go AWOL," Helen said. "Orestis, pop along to her cabin, would you? Just to make sure she's all right. The ship is really rocking today. It can take the most seasoned sailor by surprise."

"Actually, I saw her about half an hour ago," Oliver said, pushing to the front. "Heading up top. She did look pretty rough, like she was about to hurl her guts up."

"She was perfectly fine when I left her," Terry said firmly. "Anouska wouldn't get sea sick."

"I'm just saying what I saw," Oliver snapped. "And she looked dog rough."

"Perhaps she's gone for a breath of fresh air," Helen said. "It's understandable. We'll start without her. Anouska can do this kind of thing in her sleep."

Time was tight. They had one opportunity to run the whole show. For the in-house crew, it was a breeze, with routines they were all well used to. Helen stepped in with a bombastic rendition of *Come Rain or Come Shine*. What her voice lacked in subtlety it made up for in volume. If the ship's fog horn ever stopped running she would make an impressive substitute.

Terry breezed through a camper than camp version of *Copacabana* then Elijah stepped forward for a sketchy version of his routine. Most of the material worked off a rapport between him and the audience and there was only so much he could prepare in advance.

Daniel came next with a three-song set. Elijah sat at the front of the stage and observed with an enormous grin on his face. He felt like a proud father. Daniel made it look and sound effortless. Elijah knew different. It required a lot of work to make something appear so easy. And a huge amount of talent.

They finished the show with everyone getting back on stage to perform *That's What Friends Are For*. Elijah was familiar enough with the chorus and that was all he needed to know. The house singers dealt with the verses, leaving Elijah and Daniel to sing along with the main section.

The entire rehearsal went without a hitch.

Apart from Anouska's absence.

"Got to love you and leave you for the time being," Daniel said as they left the stage. "I have to get ready for this afternoon."

"I'll miss you," Elijah said, planting both of his hands on Daniel's arse and pulling him in for a kiss.

"You won't have time to miss me. The show starts at two-thirty."

"I'll be here."

"Front row this time," Daniel said, moving a hand inside his T-shirt to stroke the small of his back. "I want to see you when I sing."

"You got it." Gooseflesh prickled all over Elijah's back as Daniel touched him.

"What are you going to do with yourself until then?"

"I'm gonna track down Anouska. See that she's okay. I don't believe she's sea sick. She's got the constitution of a merchant sailor. Whatever is wrong, it must be more serious."

* * * *

A mighty wind howled across Deck Sixteen. The sun beds were stacked and tied securely. There would be no bathing today. A few hardy souls braced a circuit of the deck, heads down, hair and clothes streaming behind them. The motion of the ship was bigger up here, both front and back and side to side.

There was no land in sight in any direction.

The *Atlantic Anthem*, all one-hundred-seventy tons of her, was an insignificant blip on the ocean from which she took her name.

Elijah paused in the full force of the wind, gripping tight to the handrail, and gave himself a moment to appreciate the beauty of nature and of where he was. The boat lurched beneath his feet and the wind tore at his hair — an exhilarating feeling.

Maybe because he was in love, all his impressions were heightened. He felt part of the elements. Part of this vast rolling seascape. He wished Daniel was with him at that moment to be part of this with him.

He was already looking forward to the future. To all the adventures they could have. To traveling and making memories. New memories they would experience together.

Elijah smiled into the wind. *You're getting carried away.* It was nice all the same.

He set off along the deck, checking for Anouska. He doubted he would find her up here, especially in this weather, but it was worth a complete turn of the deck, just to be sure. He'd already visited her cabin and all the backstage areas he might expect to find her.

Missing rehearsal was thoroughly out of character for such a professional. For her to bail without a word of explanation, something had to be wrong.

She hadn't reported to the sick bay. Terry had said there

was nothing amiss when they'd met a few hours earlier. She had been looking forward to this evening — the last time the current crew would all be together. So where was she?

She couldn't have vanished, not on a ship like this.

Elijah's gaze was drawn back to the water. It was awfully rough out there. He had a swift and irrational sense of dread. What if...? *No, it's ludicrous. Anouska has years of experience at sea. She couldn't have fallen overboard.*

Could she?

No way, he told himself. He was being a drama queen. She had to be here. He would find her.

He had to keep looking.

Chapter Thirteen

Oliver strode along the passenger corridor of Deck Ten as if he had every right to be there. He wore a baseball cap with the bill pulled low over his face and a T-shirt he had snatched from the laundry. It was vital to act natural, like he was a passenger heading back to his cabin. Nothing out of the ordinary. If he didn't attract attention, no one would give him a second glance. And if any of the security cameras picked him up, he would be unrecognizable.

Anouska's corpse was stashed safely out of sight, inside a large suitcase, stowed beneath his bed. Getting her into the case had been easy enough. Freshly dead, her body had been loose and malleable and her slim dancer's figure fit inside with room to spare. He packed towels around the body. He recalled reading somewhere that corpses leaked bodily fluids after so long. He couldn't take the chance of her stinking up the ship before he had time to get rid of her, so he packed it up tight.

Funny, but he had no remorse for what he'd done. Quite the opposite. He was buzzing from the incident. Better than any drug he'd taken. Better than sex. *Murder – who knew it was such a trip?*

Not that he'd set out to kill the bitch. She'd gotten in the way. Made things tough for him. She'd still be alive if she wasn't so damn nosey. Did he regret it? *No fucking way.* And if he could get rid of her without being found out, that was how it would stay.

Oliver followed the port side corridor toward the stern. His luck held out. He hadn't passed a single passenger since getting out of the lift. Not that they would recognize him if he did. Oliver had a performer's skill for turning it on and off. When he wanted to act like a star, he could be larger than life. The center of attention. But when he wished to go unseen that was easy too. With his head down and shoulders slouched, he appeared totally nondescript. Not exactly invisible but plain enough to avoid attention.

He was a natural actor.

Maybe that was what he should do when this was all over. Get into acting. He could be the new Eddie Redmayne or Ben Whishaw. Why not? He was better looking than either of them. Sexier. It would be easy.

Singing on these cruises — it was a dead-end job. For losers like Daniel and Vladislav. He knew better than that. He was a killer. He could do anything he wanted to. Nobody would stop him.

Around the next turn, he found what he wanted. A house-keeping trolley laden with sheets, towels and toilet rolls had been positioned outside an open stateroom door.

Oliver smiled slyly to himself. Another perfect plan coming together.

Inside the stateroom, a young Filipino housekeeper had finished making up the bed and was straightening the living area. Like most of the Filipinos on board, Benjie was slightly built with an amiable nature. Oliver couldn't stand them, any of them. There were too many foreigners on this ship. And if his race wasn't bad enough, Benjie was a housekeeper. The lowest of the low when it came to members of crew.

Benjie had had the hots for Oliver since he came on board. His eyes came out on stalks whenever Oliver walked past. Tongue practically hanging out. As if he'd have any interest in a little munchkin like that. *No way.*

Until now.

From zero to hero, little Benjie was about to become extremely useful.

Oliver checked that there was no one in the corridor to see him before he slipped inside the cabin and shut the door.

Benjie looked up, surprised.

"Hello, sir," he said in the bright, overly cheerful voice these house-rats were programmed to use when speaking to the passengers. So bloody contrived. They only did it to secure themselves a fat tip at the end of the voyage. *Creeps.*

Oliver removed his cap. Benjie's smile faltered when he realized he wasn't the occupant of the room.

"Mr. Oliver, sir. What are you doing here?"

Oliver gave a smoldering look. That would get his little pecker hard in an instant. "I'm looking for you, Benjie," he said in a deep, sexy voice.

The housekeeper's eyes widened. "Sir... I don't understand."

"I think you do," Oliver said, taking a significant step toward him. *Silly little rice queen, he looks like he's about to have a heart attack.* "It's the last day. We might not see each other after tomorrow. Not ever. We can't let this opportunity go to waste."

Benjie's gaze flickered all over the room before returning to Oliver. He looked petrified. "We could get in a lot of troubles."

"Benjie, trust me. *No one* will ever know about this."

Oliver fell to his knees and made for Benjie's crotch. He eased his trousers around his ankles and took his stiff little dick into his mouth. One of Oliver's special blow jobs. It took hardly any effort to reduce Benjie to a gasping, quivering wreck. *Who can resist the best cocksucker at sea?*

As he skillfully sucked Benjie's small cock, Oliver lifted the access key from his trousers and slid it into his back pocket.

* * * *

The show went like a dream as Daniel performed to another packed house. Maximum capacity. Most of the passengers overcame their sea sickness and made it to the theater for his matinee. While the ship rolled on turbulent seas, he tried to take their minds off it. He worked the bumpy ride into his act, making a joke of it, spinning an exceptionally violent roll into a prat fall which got the whole auditorium laughing.

Laughter and song—they were guaranteed to make anyone feel better.

The front row was packed with familiar faces. Elijah sat on the aisle seat, smiling proudly, looking so damned handsome. There were a variety of fans who'd approached him for selfies and autographs in the last two days. He spotted the Robshaw family, Julieann and her parents, having a good time. Half way through the show he noticed Terry, three rows back. That took him by surprise. More so to see Terry enjoying himself. Maybe the old guy was mellowing toward him.

He put on a great show. Daniel was on top form. He knew it. From the first song, he nailed it.

There was no real structure to the set. He had scribbled the final song list on a sheet of A4 and passed it to the band leader half an hour before the show. It was informal and relaxed. An eclectic mix of songs he'd performed throughout his career. There were stories attached, about shows he'd appeared in or jobs he'd failed to get. He had a simple, self-deprecating way of telling an anecdote that went down well with the crowd.

He closed the show with *All Over the World*. A big gamble. He hoped Oliver wasn't sitting somewhere in the dark, waiting to take offense. It seemed unlikely. Oliver hated him so much, he couldn't imagine why he'd come to his show. But it was an important song and he wanted to sing it.

"So, this is the very first song I ever recorded. The first song I ever sang professionally. It's always been a favorite of mine, even if I didn't do it justice all those years ago. Hopefully, I'll put that right this afternoon."

The band played a version based on the original ELO track and not Overload's tacky cover. It was a smash. Despite the weather, the audience was on their feet before he finished the first verse. The theme of the song struck a chord. It was the last day and everybody wanted to join the party. When he concluded, the applause was deafening.

Daniel took a bow.

"Oh, wow," he gasped breathlessly, staggered by the response. "I can't thank you enough for that. Honestly. You've been brilliant. Each one of you. Now, get out there and enjoy what's left of your holiday. And don't forget to join us back here tonight for the finale. It will be terrific fun. I promise."

With the applause still resounding, he left the stage. He'd have gladly performed another set. Given them what they wanted for the rest of the afternoon. When a show went as well as that, he never wanted it to end.

He'd hardly had time to grab a towel and wipe the sweat from his brow before Elijah joined him in the dressing room. He took him into his arms and hugged him tight.

"Congratulations," Elijah gasped. "That was amazing. I don't think you have any idea how great you were. You smashed it. The people sat next to me were going crazy. They loved every minute of it."

Daniel hugged him back. "I loved it too."

"I could tell," Elijah nuzzled the small of his neck, planting a soft kiss.

"You don't think I went too far with that last song? I genuinely wanted to sing it but was concerned I might put Oliver's nose out."

"He doesn't own the song. I doubt he remembers it or that he was even there. I saw him on Deck Five about ten minutes before the show. I was looking for Anouska."

"What? Hasn't she turned up yet?"

Elijah stepped back, shaking his head. "Oliver reckoned he'd seen her. That she was sea sick. He says he gave her some pills and she went to lie down."

The look on his face made it evident Elijah had doubts. "Do you think he's lying?"

He shrugged. "My gut instinct says yes. I don't trust him. He acts so bloody suspiciously all the time."

"I know what you mean. He's got that kind of face and a bad attitude. But why would he lie about this? It's not like he has anything to gain."

"God knows. I called by her cabin before the show but there was no answer. I didn't want to knock too hard, in case she was really sick and asleep. But... I don't know. I've got no reason to be suspicious either. She probably is ill with the way this ship is tossing about. It's just strange that no one other than Oliver has seen her."

As if to prove the point, the *Anthem* listed sharply to one side before correcting herself.

"If he did give her those pills," Daniel said, "she might not have heard you knocking. She could be sleeping it off."

Elijah sighed. "I'll give it another hour and knock again. If that doesn't work, I'll track down her roommate and get her to check. If anything has happened... If she fell overboard, in this weather she wouldn't stand a chance."

Daniel put his arms around Elijah and hugged him tight. "You're a good friend but you worry too much. Anouska knows her way around a ship. She wouldn't do anything dangerous or take a risk. There's no way could she fall overboard. She'll be on board somewhere."

Elijah hugged back, pressing his face into Daniel's neck. "You're right. I know."

"There is another possibility. I wouldn't say anything in front of the others. Not yet, 'cause if it's true she could get in trouble. But maybe she's found someone. You know, a passenger. This being the last day and all, they could be holed up a stateroom together having a hell of a good time."

"That's not likely. She wouldn't miss a show for a guy. At the very least she'd have contacted Helen to say she was sick. Made an excuse."

"Try not to worry. She'll turn up."

Elijah ran his hand down the small of Daniel's back and nuzzled his ear with his lips. Daniel's flesh prickled from the top of his head to his feet. Elijah had a magic touch. He electrified Daniel's entire body whenever they made contact.

"This is nice," Elijah murmured.

"Sure is," Daniel said, slipping his hands beneath Elijah's T-shirt, caressing his hot skin. He moved to the base of his spine. Finding access to the back of his jeans, he slid his hand inside, going straight into his underpants to the cleft of his arse.

"Cheeky," Elijah sighed, turning his head for a kiss.

Daniel pressed his lips softly on top of Elijah's, teasing with the tip of his tongue before pressing inside for a full open-mouthed kiss. He had both hands down the back of Elijah's pants, parting his cheeks with one hand while the other located his hot opening. It responded instantly to his touch. Elijah pushed his hips back against his fingers.

Passion consumed them both.

Elijah quickly unfastened his pants and shoved them to his ankles, allowing Daniel unrestricted access to his arse. Daniel pulled his body tight against him while his fingers teased and caressed his sensitive hole. He knew just what to do. Where to touch him, how much pressure to apply. It amazed him how quickly they'd become attuned to each other's bodies. Elijah's muscle melted. Resistance gone. Daniel slid a finger deep into his hot core.

All cares were forgotten. They had no time to bolt the door.

Daniel lifted Elijah onto the dressing table and drew his butt to the edge, angling it into a perfect position. He sheathed his cock in a condom and fingered lube into Elijah's passage. Elijah clutched the table and hitched his arse upward, opening himself wider. Daniel wanted him. All of him.

They let out a long collective sigh as Daniel slipped inside. Smoothly, effortless, he went all the way. Daniel leaned forward and wrapped his arms around Elijah.

They were made for this. Nothing had ever felt better.

Chapter Fourteen

"That's the finest voice I've ever heard."

"Smooth as Baileys."

"I could listen to him all day."

The acclaim wouldn't stop. Oliver heard it all over the ship. Daniel Blake had taken the damn place by storm. These people had evidently lost their minds. It must be the weather, making them soft in the head, lowering their expectations. *So he can carry a tune. Big deal. He isn't that good.* Oliver hadn't intended to watch the matinee. He had more vital things to do. Like getting rid of a corpse. But curiosity got the better of him. More like a morbid fascination. He didn't want to see the show. Didn't *want* to hear Daniel sing. None the less, he lurked at the back of the theater to catch the last fifteen minutes of his act.

The purple rinse brigade rolled in their seats, laughing at his anecdotes. *What the fuck? When did this dickhead become funny?* The crowd lapped it up. They were so easily pleased. This kind of act could be found in any Blackpool pub, any day of the week. It was nothing special. The motion of the ship was definitely affecting people's judgment. And taste.

"So, this is the very first song I ever recorded," Daniel announced at the end of the show.

Oliver couldn't believe it. No way. No fucking way. He couldn't sing *that* song. But the bastard did. *All Over the World*, the song *he* recorded first, the song that should have launched his pop career. The audacity of the fucker. It was a deliberate attack. Daniel sticking two fingers up to Oliver. Lording it over him because of his headline status. It shouldn't have been such a shock. Behind the smarmy image and nice guy façade, Daniel Blake was a bitter, insecure and untalented twat.

He murdered the number. Big surprise. It had flopped the first time he sang it and sounded no better now.

He would get what was coming to him. And soon. Very soon. But first, Oliver had a bigger problem to solve.

Getting rid of Anouska.

He had stolen the door pass from the horrid little housekeeper. That would grant him access to all the passenger staterooms on Deck Ten. He could still taste Benjie's foul semen at the back of his throat but it had been worth it. The over-excited Filipino had come in less than a minute, so giving him a blow job was no real hardship. And he'd gotten the pass key as a result.

If only the rest of his plan was so straightforward.

The interior of the ship was swamped with passengers. As a storm raged outside, they stuck to the main decks and their staterooms. The elevators were busy all day, giving him little opportunity to haul a heavy suitcase through the lobby and up to Ten. He realized his best chance would occur during Daniel's show when around nine hundred people would pack into the theater.

Oliver had chosen Deck Ten for a good reason. Oh, yes. He knew exactly which stateroom Anouska was destined for.

He went back to his own room where the corpse remained hidden beneath his bed.

His fat, greasy roommate lay belly up in bed like a beached whale.

"What are you still doing in your pit?" Oliver hissed.

"I'm sick," his roommate moaned. "It's this motion. I can't take it. Thank God we'll be on dry land this time tomorrow."

Idiot.

Oliver considered whether to drag the case from under the bed right then. It was the last day, so getting out a suitcase wouldn't look that unusual. Taking it out of the cabin while all of his stuff still hung in the wardrobe was another matter. His roommate was probably too stupid to catch on but he couldn't take the risk.

He didn't need it.

Anouska's absence had already been noticed.

Elijah Mann was asking a lot of questions. Oliver hadn't realized they were such good friends. He'd fobbed him off twice by saying he'd just seen her but doubted the comedian would fall for it a third time. He'd looked suspicious when he'd fed him the line about her going for a lie down.

Who knew the silly bitch was so popular?

Why did everything have to be so difficult?

This fucking job had turned out to be the biggest mistake of his life. One shit storm after another. He didn't deserve this.

Something had to go right for him soon. He headed back to the promenade.

"He's so handsome, isn't he?"

"He looks great on television but he's so much sexier in real life."

Conversation came at Oliver from every direction. The stupid bastards were still babbling about Daniel. They were half cut, most of them. Taking advance of their all-inclusive drinks packages for one last time, they knocked back beers, spirits and cocktails like it was the end of the world. Maybe Daniel sounded better when Oliver was pissed.

They would be talking a different story later this evening. Praise for Daniel Blake would not be so grand following the finale. He'd make sure of that.

Anouska might have knocked the timing of his sabotage off course but he still intended to see it through. Daniel would regret everything he'd ever stolen from Oliver.

It was payback time.

* * * *

At six o'clock, Captain Rassimov made an unscheduled

passenger announcement over the public address system. For the duration of the cruise, he'd addressed the guests promptly at ten each morning, keeping them abreast of their location and weather conditions. When the P.A. gave off its chime at six, almost all the passengers stopped what they were doing to listen.

"Good evening, ladies and gentlemen. Good evening, crew." The captain spoke slowly and calmly in his thick Italian accent. It was important for everyone to understand what he was about to say. "As you will have noticed the ship is moving around in the water this evening."

Nervous laughter carried through the public areas. Drinks were raised to steady uneasy nerves.

"Please do not be alarmed. We have been tracking this weather front for several days and it is nothing that we did not expect. For a ship like the *Atlantic Anthem* this is nothing to be concerned about. Nothing we have not encountered before. However, your safety and comfort are our number one priority. This is why I am speaking to you now. To reassure you and offer some precautionary advance.

"For most of today we have followed a course slightly different to our initial schedule. This has been to avoid the worst of the storm conditions. We have navigated further out into the Atlantic Ocean to sail around the eye of the storm, which currently sits in the North of Biscay and the English Channel."

A hush fell over the passengers. This sounded serious.

"In order to ensure the most comfortable conditions for you today we are now around three hours behind schedule. Again, this is nothing to be concerned about. However, as you all know, we cannot avoid the English Channel for much longer if we are to get home. We will be entering those waters around midnight. We'll do everything we can to ensure your comfort but a certain amount of motion will be unavoidable.

"Please take the greatest care when you move around the ship. For your safety, the open areas of the deck will be locked. We ask that you keep your balcony doors closed and use the handrails at all times. Take your time. Please look after each other. Speak to our wonderful crew for any assistance you may require. I want each and every one of you to enjoy your last night on board this beautiful ship. All of the bars and restaurants remain open and we have a spectacular finale in the main theater. There is much out there for you to enjoy.

"The weather conditions may concern some of you. Rest assured, this vessel is more than capable of handling this and we should be in calmer water around three a.m. Until then, take care and have a wonderful last night on board the *Atlantic Anthem*."

* * * *

Before any show the backstage area was a flurry of activity. Technicians rushed around with walkie-talkies, making sure everything was in place. Dancers were helped into elaborate costumes and gave their faces a last-minute sweep of the makeup brush. Rails of clothing were pushed hurriedly from one dressing area to another. There was invariably an air of excitement and expectation.

Tonight it was even more noticeable. As the ship dipped in the troughs between waves only to rise at erratic angles seconds later, the backstage operation was in chaos. Brushes, bottles and glasses slid across the dressing tables, often smashing to the floor. Sick bags and buckets were strewn all around. Many of the crew were feeling ill and fighting nausea.

But the show would still go on. This was the finale. They couldn't adjourn it until tomorrow.

Elijah pushed through the debris of feathers, sick bags and scattered makeup. He wore his blue suit, his hair neatly brushed and ready for the stage.

"Has Anouska turned up yet?" he asked one of the other dancers.

"Not seen her," the girl said, sipping cautiously at a bottle of water. Beneath the heavy makeup, her face was puce.

"Has anyone? Has she reported sick?"

"Must have. Shanitta is doing her song."

Shit! Nobody had seen her all day apart from Oliver. *Why does no one else find this unusual?*

He had tried her cabin again around five. Still no answer. He had to find her roommate.

"Where's Tammy?" he urged.

"Around there," the girl replied.

He found Anouska's roommate being sewn into a sequined showgirl outfit with huge pink ostrich feathers. *It must be for Terry's* Copacabana *number.*

"I haven't seen her," Tammy said.

"Isn't she in your cabin?" he asked.

"She wasn't an hour ago. Her bed hadn't been slept in either."

"Don't you think that's odd? That no one has seen her all day? She's disappeared."

"She left a message she was sick. Shanitta is standing in tonight."

"When? When did she leave this message?"

"I dunno. She must have called it in this afternoon. She's been taken out with sea sickness once before. We hit a storm in the Med last year. She still went on but spent the whole show running for the buckets in the wings. It happens."

"Oh." That sounded reassuring at least, if she was prone to sickness in rough weather. "But don't you find it odd that nobody has seen her? Nobody all day. Where could she have gone? Does she have a boyfriend on board?"

Two dressers came forward to help Tammy into an enormous feathered tail piece. "She did have a thing with Mario, the chief engineer, earlier in the summer. I don't think it amounted to much but she could be with him. He's got a much nicer cabin than us. A proper stateroom. She's probably holed up in the there. I know I would be, if I was puking me guts up. Better do it in luxury than a shared shithole."

Elijah was somewhat reassured after talking to Tammy. It fit with Daniel's idea about her shacking up with a guy somewhere. Still, it was out of character. From what he knew of Anouska it wasn't her style. But how well *did* he really know her? No one else was concerned. Maybe he was overreacting and just being a drama queen. It wouldn't be the first time.

Still, if he could get a message to this engineer, Mario, and confirm she was with him, he would feel a lot happier.

* * * *

Oliver sat at his dressing table, one in a line of four set aside for the male singers and dancers. His hair and makeup were fixed for the show. He just needed to put on his costume for the first number. There was plenty of time. He sat in his underpants. It was too damn hot to get dressed yet.

Butterflies danced in his stomach but they had nothing to do with the show. He could play this tired routine in his sleep. He had bigger worries. Anouska's corpse was still under his bed but that didn't bother him either. He'd deal with her later.

Getting to Daniel was the priority.

If he couldn't carry through his plan, then killing Anouska would have been a waste of time. There were scores to settle.

The drugged bottle of water stood on Oliver's table. All he had to do was get it into Daniel's room. This was his last chance. Thanks to Anouska, he'd missed out on the opportunity to ruin the matinee. If he failed now, that would be it. He wanted to degrade his rival in public. That was what really counted. Seeing Daniel fail in front of an audience, a full house at that, would be the ultimate reward. It was what his dreams were made of.

Getting the bottle into Daniel's room without drawing

suspicion was easier said than done. There were too many people around now.

He watched the dressing room door though his mirror. Daniel was in there now. He thought about entering, under some kind of pretense. He could say he wanted to offer an olive branch, put the past behind them, but Daniel wouldn't fall for that. And there was still no way to get the bottle in there without him noticing. If Daniel caught him with the water, he was unlikely to drink it. And if he did, he'd know what had happened as soon as he felt ill.

Why did I think this would be easy?

Oliver watched and waited. He had to be patient just a little longer.

He saw Elijah reflected in the mirror, heading for Daniel's door. *Damn it.* If he was in there, he'd never get the bottle through. Elijah paused for a moment, staring at Oliver in the glass. *Tosser.* What a waste of space he'd turned out to be. He'd had such potential when he showed up the other day, so sexy and funny. A breath of fresh air after all these cruise ship cunts. Oliver had set his eye on him, sure they would enjoy some hot, dirty sex during their last few days at sea. But no, the fucker had terrible taste and had latched onto Daniel instead. And then today, asking all these bloody questions about Anouska. He was still at it. Just a few minutes ago he'd heard him looking for her roommate, Tammy.

Why couldn't he let it go?

Didn't he get it? Nobody gave a shit.

Oliver stood up and stretched. Showing off his body in nothing but a black thong. His clearly delineated ribs, his tattoos, his piercings. He ran a hand over his hot little arse. *That's right, fool, get a good look at what you're missing. How does Daniel compare to that?*

Elijah stared emotionlessly at his reflection before opening the door to Daniel's room and disappearing inside.

Fuck off then. You won't get another chance from me.

Terry St. King came skulking past in a pair of mauve

trousers with a sequined waistcoat and top hat. His eyes tightened as he looked Oliver up and down.

"Don't stare at what you can't afford," Oliver said. He stuck out his flat buttocks. That would give the old coot something to jerk over when he got back to his cabin tonight.

Terry twisted his face. "Put some clothes on, darling, before one of the dressers mistakes you for a hat pin."

Oliver puffed out his chest. What did this emaciated troll know? "I'm more man than you ever were, you poisonous sack of bones."

Terry snorted. "You silly boy. You're not a *man*. From the little I've seen of you this last month, I doubt you're even human."

How dare he?

Terry was a two-faced bitch, like everyone else in this crew.

"What would you know?" Oliver bristled.

"I know your days are numbered. Enjoy the show tonight. I don't think we'll be seeing much more of you."

"You nasty old prick," he howled as Terry departed.

Without a backward glance, Terry flipped him two fingers.

Bastard. They all were. He didn't want to see any of them ever again. He couldn't wait to get off this ship and go back to a normal life. Real life.

If he had to tour the clubs of Northern clubs till he was a hundred, it would be better than this shit. Better than finishing up like Terry — a has-been nobody wanted around. That was a frightening thought. No, he'd never end up like that sad bastard.

Vladislav came up to the dressing table next to him. He wore his full costume for the opening number, a ghastly hot-pink Lycra shirt and tight black pants that left nothing to the imagination. The Russian hung to the left. He looked disapprovingly at Oliver. "You are not dressed. It is almost time."

"What can I say, Vlad? Some of us don't require as long as

others to get ready."

The Russian frowned. "Why does everything you say have to be so rude? It's not nice."

Oliver laughed. "Not nice! You got off easy. I haven't even started on you. If I wanted to be mean to you, you would definitely know it."

"I think you have been mean to everyone."

"Boo hoo."

He headed to the dressing rail to pick up his crappy costume. Everyone was so sensitive around here. None of them got him. He'd only been on board a few weeks and he'd been on his best behavior for most of that. He hadn't been horrible to anyone, not really. Well, Anouska. But that was different. She'd gotten in the way of his revenge.

And on that front, time was running out.

He had to do something about it fast. Like now.

Fully dressed, he returned to his dressing table. There was nothing else for it. He would have to go in and pretend he wanted to make amends for the past. Somehow or other he had to get that bottle to him.

But the bottle was not where he'd left it. Oliver's heart leapt.

"Where's my water? I put it right here," he screeched.

"Sorry. I was thirsty. I'll get you another." Vladislav sat at the next dressing table with the empty bottle in his hand. "That tasted weird. Maybe it stood around too long. I'll get us two cool ones."

Oliver stared in disbelief.

Why does nothing go right?

Chapter Fifteen

The evening show proved to be another success. Daniel and Elijah watched from the wings as the singers and dancers went through the opening number. Ordinarily Daniel would have waited in the dressing room until he got the call for his turn. But tonight, he wanted to experience the whole event. The theater was packed. Though the ship rolled violently with the storm, it didn't deter the crowds. Earlier in the voyage, the passengers might have retired to their staterooms but this evening all anyone wanted to do was enjoy themselves.

The dancers coped admirably with the shifting stage. Even from his position at the side, standing still, Daniel twice lost his balance. If Elijah hadn't been there to catch him, he would have gone over. The fact that no one had broken any bones could only be a miracle.

Elijah slipped a hand around Daniel's waist, holding him near. He could get used to this. Being close to Elijah, being held by him, there was nothing he wanted more. Daniel slid his hand around Elijah, gently mirroring the action. They were good together. So easy.

"Vladislav looks like he might be suffering from the effects of the sea," Elijah whispered.

They were coming to the end of the first number. There had been nothing about his performance to give it away, no missed steps, ill-judged lifts or mistakes, but his face was a giveaway. Trying to paste on the regulatory smile, Vlad only succeeded in looking more ill.

"Poor guy," Daniel whispered. "At least he's putting the effort in."

The dancers left the stage in a rush, dashing for the next costume change. As Vladislav walked past, Daniel realized just how sick he was. His skin was waxen, like a pale and sweaty corpse. He stumbled as a swift wave forced the ship to the left. Daniel caught him before he went over.

"Easy," he said, helping the Russian to stand straight. Vladislav's pupils were like black saucers. Wet hair stuck to his forehead. He blazed like a furnace. "Maybe you should sit the rest of the show out. You could get hurt out there."

"No," he answered. "I am fine. Have never missed a performance. I'll not quit with less than an hour to go."

With a discernible effort, he pulled himself together and hastened to the changing area.

Helen took to the stage, whipping the already excited crowd into a frenzy. "We can weather any storm on the *Atlantic Anthem*," she hollered proudly. "Because we know how to party." The band blared on queue and Helen burst into her bombastic version of *Come Rain or Come Shine*, sounding bigger and brassier than the number she'd rehearsed.

He sneaked a peek into the auditorium and every person out there was on their feet. "She knows how to give it some," he said, genuinely impressed.

"She's really something," Elijah said. "She runs this place with minute precision and still sings like *that*."

Daniel and Elijah stepped aside as the dancers came back through. They were dressed in even more outlandish showgirl outfits for their routine with Terry. The boys had changed into tight black trousers and Cuban shirts which were open to the navel.

"Shit, look at Vlad now," Elijah said.

He stood toward the back of the group, seeming worse than ever. His eyelids were drooping and his mouth has a downturned cast.

"It looks worse than sea sickness," Daniel said.

On stage Helen announced Terry to the crowd. The music struck up, and the dancers made their entrances. Vladislav stumbled forward and almost got as far as the stage. Daniel saw what was about to happen as his face glazed over. He stopped dead in his track and swayed for a moment on the unstable deck. Then he went down, face forward.

Daniel reached him just in time. He slid his elbows beneath Vlad's armpits, taking the weight to ease him to the floor.

The show continued without him. On stage, the other dancers were oblivious to his collapse.

"Help me turn him over," Daniel said.

Elijah got down beside him and they rolled him onto his back. "What happened?"

Daniel put his cheek close to Vlad's mouth and laid a palm on his chest, feeling for breath. The ribcage rose minutely against his hand. "He's breathing. Very slightly, but he is." He shook Vlad's shoulders and called his name, mouth close to his ear. No response. He was out cold. Daniel shuffled round to Vlad's lower half, raised his feet and placed them on top of his own knees. If he had only fainted, the elevation should bring him around soon.

"What's going on?" Helen tottered off the stage, practically falling over them.

"He passed out," Elijah said. "Just now."

"But he looked sick as dog before that. When he came off stage, he was ghastly."

"I spoke to him just before the show," Helen said. "He was fine then. Looking forward to it, in fact."

"Whatever happened, it came on quick," Daniel said.

"Food poisoning?" Elijah suggested.

"He'd have said something earlier." Helen leaned in closer. "God, he looks awful. Like a corpse."

Daniel was worried. There was no sign of him of coming round. This was more than a faint. "You'd better get a medic. We'll take him to the dressing room."

With Elijah's help, he carried Vlad to his room. There was no bed or sofa, so they laid him on the floor. He checked his pulse and breathing again. Still okay. Daniel placed him in the recovery position.

Elijah's brow furrowed. "Doesn't look good, does he?"

"No, but he's breathing. That's the main thing." He was trained in first aid and resuscitation though he'd never had to use it. He'd hoped he never would.

"You don't think...it's something going round the dancers? First Anouska takes ill, now Vlad. More than a coincidence, don't you think?"

"Could be. I don't know. Perhaps if they both ate the same thing. But this isn't food poisoning. He would be stuck in the bathroom if that's all it was. Has anyone checked on Anouska?"

"I don't know. I haven't spoken to anyone who's actually seen her. Except that arsehole Oliver. Even her friend, Tammy, who heard she'd phoned in sick, wasn't sure who she spoke to."

"You sound worried."

"I am," Elijah said. "I've had a bad feeling about this all day. It doesn't sit right with me. No one should disappear for a whole day. Especially not someone with an excellent sick record."

Orestis came to the door. "Elijah, you're on in a minute."

"You're joking. I can't go on stage now. After this."

"It's all right," Daniel said softly. "The medic will be here soon. I'll stay with him. I can handle it till they get here. There's nothing you can do besides your show. It must go on, remember?"

His shook his head. "I really don't like it."

"He'll be fine. Don't worry. Go and give those passengers a night to remember. They deserve it."

* * * *

Being funny wasn't easy, not with so much on his mind, but Elijah did his best. Daniel was right—the passengers did deserve it. They'd invested a lot of money on their cruise and entertainment was a big part of the package. What went on behind the scenes didn't concern them. The finale couldn't be an anti-climax. He walked out with a smile and launched into his routine. With eight minutes to fill, he kept it short and snappy.

The first few rows were filled with familiar faces which made it easy to engage. A lot of people there he'd come to recognize as Daniel's fans.

Thankfully they laughed in all the right places.

He made gentle fun of Helen and her infatuation with Captain Rassimov, then did an impression of the captain, mimicking his Italian accent and the grave tone of his daily announcements. The audience loved it. The way the ship tossed on the mountainous waves had rattled the strongest of nerves and they needed a release. Laughter was the greatest cure.

Except for himself.

The smile vanished the second he left the stage.

Daniel waited in the wings.

"How's Vlad now?" he asked.

"Still out," Daniel answered. "The doctor is with him."

"Does anyone know what happened yet?"

"Too early to say. I'm sure he'll be all right. He's still breathing, that's the main thing."

Helen announced Daniel and it was his turn to take the stage. Elijah loitered at the side. If the doctor was busy with Vlad, he'd be better out the way. No point interfering. But before he left, he wanted to speak to the medic about Anouska.

Daniel delivered another great set. The passengers couldn't get enough of him. Despite having already performed a full concert that afternoon his voice was in top form.

Even Elijah forgot his worries for fifteen minutes. Daniel had the ability to make everyone in the crowd feel good.

He seized him as soon as he came off, enveloping him in a tight hug. *So proud.*

"My God, you were incredible again. Just incredible. I don't know how you do it."

Daniel hugged back, pressing his face against the side of Elijah's neck. "I had to finish on a high. It's the closure I wanted when I came back to sea. Oh wow, it was incredible. What an audience."

The double whammy of Elijah's act followed by Daniel had the crowd in rapture. Just as well, because what came next was stupendously awful.

It was another group number for the *Anthem* company. Vladislav should have sung lead vocal. With no other option, Oliver Gill was thrust into the role of understudy.

"What?" Elijah heard him complain. "I hardly know that song."

"Yes, you do," Orestis told him firmly. "Now get out and do it."

With the band already playing the intro and the first dancers taking to the stage, Oliver had no choice but to do what he was told. The song was Take That's *Rule the World*, a favorite with the audience. Their arms were raised and swaying with the music as he entered. Then Oliver opened his mouth and started in the wrong key. He tried to correct it but there was no coming down. The song got worse as he went along, strangling every note. When he reached the chorus, his voice was a painful screech.

"I shouldn't laugh," Daniel said, staring wide-eyed at the car crash on stage.

"Laugh away," Elijah said. "If anyone deserves to make an arse of themselves it's him. He had this coming."

The audience laughed too. The final applause was a combination of ridicule and sympathetic clapping.

Oliver gave Daniel a vicious look as he stormed off stage.

"I must have done something to deserve that," Daniel said.

"You were better than him. Though he shouldn't hold that against you. Everyone on that stage is better than him. It couldn't have happened to a nicer person."

Helen called the performers back for the final group number. Elijah and Daniel stood together, close to the front, for *That's What Friends Are For*. The audience were on their feet, loving every minute. Elijah smiled and waved and made eye contact with as many of them as he could.

At last, the show was over.

* * * *

Terry St. King was in Daniel's dressing room, picking up the cushions and towels they had been used to make Vladislav comfortable. His face was drawn and troubled. Daniel had never seen him look so old and frail. He wished he'd been nicer to the old guy. The spikey exterior he showed ninety-five percent of the time was clearly just a front.

"Where's Vlad?" Daniel asked.

"They've taken him to the medical bay," Terry answered. "A few minutes ago."

"Did the doctor say what's wrong with him?"

With a sigh, Terry pulled out a chair and sat. "They think he might have been drugged."

"Drugged?"

Terry nodded, thin-lipped. "That's what the man said. They won't know for sure until they test his blood. I'm not sure they even have the facilities for those kinds of tests on board, but that's what he seemed to think."

"Was Vlad a drug user?" Elijah asked.

There was a short silence before Terry said, "I very much doubt it. You'd be mad to in this job. The policy is zero tolerance. If you were caught, you'd be finished. Possessing drugs on a ship is an international offense. Besides, he seemed like such a clean-living boy. Always in the gym when he wasn't working. Very careful about what he ate. I just can't see him using that shit."

"No," Elijah said, grim faced. "I can't either. But to collapse like that, in the middle of a show."

Drugs. People had to be crazy to use them but plenty did. Especially in show business. Daniel had never figured out why many performers were drawn to their artificial highs. Singing songs, hearing the audience reaction, there was no bigger thrill than that. No chemical could replicate it. He'd seen the damage drugs did at the very start of his career. Overload had played at a huge award show with dozens of other pop acts. The after-show party had been wild. He'd been sitting at the next table when a young female popstar had collapsed. She was an idol to millions of kids and her first two singles had reached number one. He'd heard she'd been using cocaine and GHB. She'd looked like she was dead when they'd stretchered her out. It was the scariest thing he'd ever seen. If he'd ever been tempted to dabble in substances, it was forgotten after that night.

He could still remember her face. Her waxen skin. Shining with cold sweat.

It was just like Vladislav.

Daniel's mind started working overtime.

"Hang on," he said, angry with himself. *Why didn't I make the connection before?* "GHB. I once saw someone OD on the stuff. She looked just like Vladislav. Same pallor, same symptoms."

"Yes," Terry said. "The doctor mentioned GHB. Rohypnol too. It could be either."

"Shit," Elijah said. "I don't like this. We need to speak to Helen. I want to know where Anouska is."

* * * *

Daniel, Elijah and Terry crammed into Helen's office. She sat behind her desk and listened to their story, remaining silent throughout and, to Daniel's relief, she took them seriously.

"Have you actually spoken to Anouska today?" Elijah asked.

"No," she said. "I haven't."

"But she called in sick. Who *did* she speak to?"

Helen looked perturbed. "I don't know. I just got a

message to say she wouldn't be on tonight."

Elijah sighed. "Damn it, no one on this fucking ship has seen or heard from her all day, apart from Oliver."

"And I wouldn't believe one word that comes out of his mouth," Terry said dryly.

"No," Helen said. "Me neither."

"Tammy mentioned a boyfriend," Elijah continued. "A maintenance manager. Mario, I think she said his name was. Any idea who that is?"

"Mario Zavaroni," Helen said. She grabbed her phone and punched in a number.

They stood, tuning in, trying to catch what the voice on the other end of the line said. They knew the worst before Helen put down the phone.

"He hasn't seen her for days," she said grimly. "They weren't that serious. They've never been an item as such."

"I didn't think so," Elijah said. "She's not mentioned him once."

Helen jabbed another number into the phone. "I'm trying her room." The phone rang and rang. Suddenly someone answered. "Anouska? Oh, Tammy. It's Helen. Is she there? Any sign of her? Okay, love. If you see or hear from her, tell her to contact me straight away. I mean that—straight away." She put down the phone. "Her bed hasn't been touched since housekeeping were in this morning."

"Fuck," Elijah said. "We should have done something straight away. We all knew it was out of character for her to go off without telling anyone."

Daniel felt powerless. "You weren't to know. Besides, Oliver said he saw her on deck."

"I don't believe him."

"Me neither," Terry said. "He's been acting weird all day. More weird than usual, that is. That boy's an off-the-scale freak."

"None of us believe him," Helen said firmly. She pressed the button for the public address system and leaned into the microphone. "This is a staff announcement. Anouska Frost and Oliver Gill to contact the Entertainment Manager's office immediately. That's Anouska Frost and Oliver Gill to contact the Entertainment Manager immediately."

They waited.

"How long do we give them?" Terry asked.

The phone rang. Helen grabbed the receiver. Their hope sank when she spoke. "Oliver."

"Shit," Elijah whispered.

Daniel put an arm on his shoulder.

"He's sticking to the same old story," she said when she hung up. "He saw her twice today and both times she complained of feeling sick. He doesn't know where she is."

"The boy is lying," Terry said.

"I think so too," Helen said sadly.

"Hang on a minute." Elijah tapped his forehead in frustration. "The first time I met Oliver, when he came onto me in the dressing room. He was high as kite. I don't know what he'd taken, but he was clearly under the influence."

"So?" Helen said.

"Oliver's dressing table is right next to Vladislav. *Who has just been hospitalized with a suspected drug overdose.* So—we know Oliver's a drug user."

"And he benefitted by getting Vlad's solo number in the finale," Daniel said.

"For what good it did," Terry sneered. "My flatulence has better tuning than that boy's voice."

"What are you saying?" Helen asked.

"I'm saying he can't be trusted. And two of your crew going down in a day is more than a coincidence. We need to find Oliver fast. And hope the bastard can lead us to Anouska before it's too late."

Chapter Sixteen

They were on to him.

The page from Helen. Then the phone call. He could hear it in her voice. She didn't believe a word he said. Somehow they'd made the connection between Anouska's disappearance and him.

He had to work fast. It wouldn't take them long to come snooping round his cabin. If they discovered her body going off in the suitcase beneath his bed, he'd be done for. But that would not happen. No way. He'd come too far. He'd see the damn thing through.

The rest of the entertainment crew were heading upstairs for the end-of-season drinks. The passengers were making their way to bed. He estimated he had a fifteen-minute window of opportunity before Helen and her band of amateur detectives came looking for him. He had to make the time count.

Oliver headed straight for the crew stairway and went down.

Nothing had gone right so far—the day had passed from bad to worse—but there was still time to turn this debacle around.

The route was clear. Good. Nobody sane would go all the way up to the Sky Lounge on foot. If he kept clear of the staff elevators he should be all right.

His head buzzed. He could use a swig of GHB to take the edge off, but the stupid Russian had swallowed the whole lot. What an idiot. The last he'd seen of him, Vladislav had been unconscious at the side of the stage. *Good.* He'd always been full of himself. It served him right. Not that he'd set out to poison Vlad. He was too insignificant — not worth the bother. Drinking the bottle intended for Daniel was one more fuckery in a day filled with them.

Vladislav might be dead. The realization dawned suddenly. He might have killed *two* people today. He wouldn't have believed it when he woke up this morning. *A double murder.* Oliver giggled. The idea wasn't as awful as it sounded. No, but it was aggravating to think he could have executed two people and Daniel still walked around.

No wonder he never won the lottery. His luck was dire.

Unlike Daniel. That fucker would come out from a sewer of shit smelling of roses. Luck had always been on his side.

Son of a bitch.

Daniel had loved it when they'd forced Oliver to replace Vlad. Unprepared, he'd died on arse in front of that full house. He'd seen the smirk on Daniel's face as he came off stage. Together with that loser Elijah. They'd been practically pissing themselves in the wings.

That was another unforeseen catastrophe. Taking Vlad's place when he collapsed. He'd have jumped at the chance any other time, in another other show. But *that* song. He'd never sung it before. With good reason. It didn't suit him. Wasn't his style. But still they'd made him do it. He'd started in the wrong key and had only gotten worse. His vocal chords had locked. Whenever he'd tried to lower his voice and rescue the number, it had risen higher and thinner. He could see the faces in the audience, laughing at him, taking the piss.

Making a mockery of him. A travesty.

Just like Daniel. That fucker should be out cold. Laid up in the sick bay. Not Vladislav.

Seething, Oliver reached Deck Two. Moving cautiously, listening, making sure he was alone, he crept toward his stateroom.

Please don't let that fat bastard still be in bed. The way his luck had gone so far, he wouldn't be surprised. But it would be unlike his roommate to miss a chance to get drunk with his band mates one last time.

Oliver opened the door and stepped inside.

Empty.

At last, something was going right.

The stench inside the cabin made him gag. It had to be Anouska. It was too early for her to have gone off just yet. The corpse must be leaking. He mustn't have packed it tight enough but he couldn't do anything about it now. He wasn't about to open the case and deal with her here. Besides, it wouldn't be long until she reached her final resting place. The bottom of the ocean. Only the fishes would smell her then.

He took a breath and caught sight of his reflection in the mirror. He looked like shit. Worse than shit. He'd had time to change into a black T-shirt and jeans but still wore his heavy stage makeup. In the ordinary light of his cabin, he looked like a sinister clown.

There was a bottle of vodka on the dresser. Exactly what he needed. He unscrewed the cap and drank straight from the bottle. Fire burned his gullet but he didn't stop. Finally fortified for the task in hand, he dropped to the floor and dragged the case from under the bed. It was much heavier than when he put it there. The smell seeping from the case was terrible this close.

What the hell? At this time of night there would be no one around to notice.

Time was running out.

He had to get rid of her and fast.

Then he could deal with his only remaining problem—Daniel.

He already had an idea about him. One that might solve all of his troubles.

* * * *

Terry arranged to meet Helen and the others on Deck Fifteen in ten minutes.

"I need to get out of these stage clothes and into something comfortable if we're going to play Nancy Drew all night," he said.

"You don't have to worry yourself, Terry. We'll let you know if anything turns up."

"Helen, dear, if you think I'm missing out on the drama, you're very much mistaken. I just need to get out of these fucking heels."

He hastened back to his cabin. He tried not to let his mask slip in front of Helen. She thought he was an insensitive old queen and he was happy to play that character. She was frightened of him and it suited him for her to be so.

But he was genuinely worried about Anouska. It was a serious matter when a member of the team went missing for over fourteen hours, whoever they were. Especially when the ship had been at sea in rough weather all that time. It was every captain's nightmare. To lose someone overboard. If Anouska didn't turn up soon they'd have to accept that likely possibility. Especially in a storm like this. What could they do for her now? She could be somewhere ten hours back in the Bay of Biscay. It was too frightful to think about.

Inside his cabin, he made a short appeal to his portrait of Princess Diana. "Please let the poor girl be on board," he said. "Let her be safe."

Anouska was a good kid. She'd offered him the kind of patience and courtesy he found rare on this ship. It was above and beyond her job to give him private coaching this morning but she had agreed without objection, seeking nothing from him in return. And despite what they suggested, she'd showed no signs of ill health this morning. She had been as fit as a fiddle.

And the only person to have sight of her afterward was Oliver Gill. That in itself was suspicious. Everything about that boy was suspicious. From the moment he'd joined the team, Terry had smelled trouble. He'd met his type before, far too frequently. What they lacked in talent they made up for in spite and bile. Jealous to the core of anyone better than them.

Terry could be a jealous bitch himself. More so as he got older. Having to watch as young men like Daniel shone in the spotlight that had once belonged to him. But the Oliver Gills of the world were far worse than Terry could ever be. A mediocre talent at best, he would never amount to much and the boy knew it. That was what made him so poisonous. Dangerous. But what had Anouska done to piss him off? He could understand it if Oliver wanted to get one over on Daniel. He was massively jealous of him. And if he was behind the business with Vladislav, that would be no surprise either. Vlad was handsome and sexy, a terrific dancer and decent little singer. Things Oliver could only dream about. But Anouska? Why?

He could worry about that later. Time was running out. It might already be too late.

Terry quickly changed out of his stage clothes into jeans, a thick black sweatshirt and sneakers.

"Wish me luck," he said to Diana and headed out the door.

The public lifts were closer to his cabin than the staff elevator. Helen would have a shit-fit if she knew he'd used them but tonight she could make an exception. Speed was crucial.

Hurrying along, Terry realized there was someone ahead of him in the crew corridor.

He heard the wheels of a trolley being drawn along the floor. It was too late to be one of the housekeepers. Alert and naturally mistrustful, Terry rose onto the balls of his feet and quickened his pace.

Rounding the passage, he saw a figure ahead.

Somebody garbed all in black was towing a large suitcase. *Well, well, well, it's Oliver.*

Terry was about to cry out and ask what he was doing when he suddenly thought better of it. It was evident from the furtive way he moved that he was up to something.

169

Why was he carrying a suitcase at this time of night? The crew weren't due to leave the ship until mid-morning. Not until all the passengers had disembarked. There was no rush to vacate their cabins. This was decidedly suspicious.

Hanging back but keeping him in sight, Terry followed.

* * * *

Oliver was out of breath. Though the suitcase had wheels, it was surprisingly heavy. How could Anouska, who'd weighed nothing in life, be so damn heavy in death?

The crew corridors were clear. His luck was holding. Reaching the door that lead to the public areas, he waited and listened. It sounded quiet enough on the other side. He opened it slowly. The door came out right beside the elevators on Deck Two. The route ahead was free. Thank God. Most of the old bastards would be in bed by now and the crew who weren't still at work would be getting drunk in the Sky Lounge.

He wheeled the case into the corridor then shut the door behind him.

Currently on Deck Fifteen, the elevator took an age to arrive. He stared at the counter as it descended, willing it to go faster. If he ran into another member of staff in the lift he would say he was helping a passenger move luggage between rooms on different levels. Anyone who knew him would know he would do nothing to help a passenger, but he counted on their indifference. As long as he didn't run into Helen or one of the cunts from her entertainment team, he'd be all right.

The elevator arrived and was empty. Luck was still on his side. If only it would hold for ten more minutes.

He dragged the case inside and hit the button for Deck Ten.

As the lift ascended, he realized just how bad the smell from the suitcase was. In this enclosed space, the stink was staggering. He could never cover it up if anyone got on board.

The elevator reached his destination without interruption.

Oliver let out a distinct breath of relief. Almost there. The nightmare was nearly over.

He dragged the case along the empty corridor. His heart beat faster, but with excitement rather than fear. Reaching his intended room, he tapped gently on the door. He was certain the cabin would be empty but waited a moment to be sure. He tapped again. No answer. Perfect.

Using the stolen access pass he unlocked the door and entered, lugging the case behind him. He slid the card into the slot which activated the lights. The large stateroom was empty. The housekeeper had already been in to turn down the bed and leave chocolates on the pillow. Everything was neat and tidy.

A polo shirt and pair of shorts were folded neatly on the sofa. He recognized them straight away. Daniel had worn them to rehearsal that morning. The room even smelled of him, of his aftershave and deodorant.

Oliver smiled. He'd made it to Daniel's stateroom undetected.

Beneath his feet the deck continued to roll up and down. The motion was much more apparent on these upper decks. Rassimov had said the storm would settle down later in the night but it showed no sign of subsiding yet.

If Oliver's luck kept up, that could also work to his advantage.

It was easy to imagine someone falling over board on a night like this. Anouska Frost was about to make a journey to the deep and if Oliver got his way, Daniel Blake would follow close behind.

* * * *

Elijah's anxiety was rising fast. Daniel could sense his concern. It was tempting to tell him not to worry, that everything would be okay, but he kept quiet. Everything was not okay. Too many things had been off this evening. Daniel barely knew Anouska, but everything he'd heard convinced him that she was a consummate professional. A hard worker who took pride in what she did. Not the kind of girl to pull a random sickie when she wanted a day off. Besides, he couldn't imagine any professional singer or dancer missing out on an end of season show. Broken bones and severe illness wouldn't keep a true artist from that stage.

Which made her disappearance all the more worrisome.

Then there was Vladislav and what had happened to him. Something was very wrong on board the ship.

The *Anthem* sick bay was located on Deck Two in the bow of the ship. The reception desk stood empty. Barring emergencies, the facilities were locked at night. There were voices coming from one of the treatment rooms. Elijah went straight up to the door, knocked once and entered without waiting.

The doctor, a small but handsome man in his early forties, dressed in evening attire, stood at the end of the bed while a young nurse took Vladislav's blood pressure. Orestis stood on the other side. His arms were crossed, with concern etched into his face. Vladislav was naked to the waist with heart monitoring equipment attached to his bare chest.

"Any change?" Elijah asked.

The doctor shook his head. "He's still out of it. Heartbeat and blood pressure are low. We're keeping an eye on him. I've taken bloods but we don't have the amenities to do a detailed test."

"Do you still believe he's suffered an overdose?" Daniel asked.

"Without a doubt," the doctor answered.

"Is Vladislav known to use drugs?" Elijah asked.

Orestis shook his head. "Quite the opposite. He's very anti-drugs. We occasionally run random tests on the dancers. His always came out clean as a whistle."

"Then he must have been spiked."

"We can't be sure of that, not until he comes round and gives his own account, but I'd say it's highly likely."

Daniel looked at Elijah. "Tell him about Oliver."

"What's this?" Orestis demanded.

Elijah told him what went down in his dressing room with Oliver on Thursday night. "He was off his tits. I don't know what he'd taken but he was high. And he sits at the dressing table next to Vlad. He's got the means and the motive. If I were to point a finger, I'd point it there."

Orestis' face clouded. "I wish you'd told me earlier. I could have run a basic test on the bastard there and then."

"You can deal with Oliver later," Daniel said. "We're more concerned about Anouska. You haven't seen her today, have you, doctor?"

"Anouska Frost," Orestis explained. "She's a member of the dance team. We've got conflicting reports about whether she is ill or missing."

"I have treated no members of the crew all day," the doctor said. "If she's ill, she hasn't been through here."

"Damn it," Elijah said. "We need to find her. No one has seen here since this morning."

"Except Oliver. I want to speak to him," Orestis said. "I want answers. Let's find the bastard, right now."

There was no reply at the door of Oliver's stateroom. Orestis pulled out his walkie-talkie and summoned one of the housekeeping supervisors to let them in. The room was empty, though the air was heavy with the stink of feces.

"It smells like something died in here," Elijah grimaced.

Orestis directed the housekeeper to open the door of Anouska's stateroom. It was also empty.

"What do we do now?" Daniel asked.

"Check out the party upstairs," Elijah said, "just in case either of them is up there. But Orestis, you and Helen need to seriously think about raising the alarm. You've got a missing member of staff. There must be measures in place for that. Something you can do."

"Let's check the party first. If we can't find them we must

speak to the captain."

"I don't like it," Elijah said. "Something should have been done hours ago."

Daniel put an arm around his shoulder. There was nothing he could say to ease Elijah's fears. As far-fetched as it sounded, he already accepted the fact that something terrible had happened to Anouska. He hoped they were wrong.

They rode together in the lift.

Daniel realized he was still wearing his stage clothes. They seemed impractical under the circumstances. He hit the button to get off on Deck Ten.

"Go to the Sky Lounge and I'll meet you there in a few minutes. I want to change into something more functional." If they had to turn the ship inside out in the search for Anouska he didn't want to do it in a shiny suit and patent leather shoes.

Elijah nodded. "Don't be long. I don't want to lose you too."

Daniel stroked his chin and leaned in for a kiss on the mouth. "Don't worry about that. You won't shake me in a hurry."

Elijah managed a weak smile. Daniel smiled back and kept it up until the doors had closed.

Then the smile collapsed. He felt ill, a sickening sensation in the pit of his stomach. Whatever they were about to discover, it would not be good. He knew that with absolute certainty. He'd experienced this same sense of dread before when his father had died.

He hurried to his room, and as he reached a turn in the corridor he walked straight into Terry. The piano singer gave a startled yelp and rounded on him.

"Oh, Daniel, it's only you," he whispered. "Thank God."

"What are you doing here?"

Terry jerked his head along the passage. "Mr. Gill. I followed him. And I might add he's acting very suspiciously. He's got a massive suitcase with him. He took it into that room there."

"Which one?"

Daniel knew the answer before Terry pointed to the door of his room. Pieces of a picture began to form in his mind. It seemed crazy, but what else was Oliver doing in there? "How did he get in?"

"He had a key," Terry whispered. "You might think I'm being an over-the-top old queen but that suitcase looked mighty heavy. You don't think...? I can hardly bring myself to say it, but after what happened to Vladislav... Anouska?"

Daniel felt a dead weight pulling at his insides. It *was* a crazy idea — Oliver dragging Anouska around in a suitcase. But why was he in his stateroom? And how come he had a key? It made little sense and yet...

Oliver Gill was nothing but trouble.

"I don't know what he's up to," Daniel said. "But it ends now. C'mon."

He drew out his key card and hurried to the door.

Chapter Seventeen

Music blasted as the lift doors opened. The party in the Sky Lounge was in full swing but neither Elijah nor Orestis were in the mood to boogie.

The ship swayed from side to side but the seasoned *Anthem* crew would not be put off by the storm. This was their last opportunity to party and they intended to take it.

"Guys." Helen scurried along the corridor from the direction of the café. "Any sign of them?"

"Nothing," Elijah said. They were running out of options.

"I've been right round the café. There's hardly anyone in there. Most of the food has been closed down. There's just the burger bar running and no one has the stomach for that."

"So if they're not in the lounge we've officially lost them?" Orestis said.

Helen nodded grimly. "In all my years at sea this has never happened."

Elijah's hopes were almost flat. They should have raised the alarm hours ago. If Anouska had fallen in the water, there'd be no chance of survival tonight. Maybe earlier, if they'd swung around in time, they might have found her. Not now. The idea of being lost on those seas was terrifying. Alone. Cold. Tired and losing strength.

An upsurge of emotion squeezed his throat. He swallowed it down. This was no time to lose it. He'd cry later if he had to. Right now, he had to keep his shit together and progress with the search.

"It'll be quicker if we split up," he said. "Helen, you go around the front of the lounge and I'll take the back.

Orestis, you go through the middle. We'll meet by the stage at the other side. If you find Anouska or Oliver, bring them with you."

They both nodded bleakly. No one expected the quest to be a success.

The party was a riot. Like an end of term blow out. It had started less than an hour earlier and already people were drunk. They danced in the aisles, on chairs, on tables. Elijah picked his way carefully around the back of the room, scrutinizing their faces, studying every group.

There were too many people he recognized without knowing them by name. Everyone was having fun. Dancing, singing, drinking. If Anouska was here they could enjoy those things together. Good friends, loved ones, colleagues.

But she wasn't.

Elijah's nerves were fraught.

Up ahead, in one of the banquettes, he spotted another familiar face. Shanitta. She danced in the company with Anouska. More importantly, she appeared to be the only friend Oliver had on the ship. The only person who tolerated him in more than the smallest dose.

Shanitta wore a few scraps of metallic material that barely made a dress. With an expanse of bare flesh on display — limbs, torso, buttocks — the outfit just about covered her tits and crotch. She looked like she was about to give a lap dance to another girlie dancer when Elijah tapped her bare shoulder.

"Hey, I'm looking for Oliver," he said.

Throwing back a mane of hair, she licked her glossy lips. "Didn't think you was interested. I 'ear you blew him off the other night."

"I need to find him."

Shanitta put her hand on his chest and murmured approval, pawing the taut muscle beneath his shirt. "Never mind Oliver. Why don't ya take a seat, sweetie, and let me give ya a nice dance. A *reeeeal* nice dance. We can even take it somewhere private if ya like." She leaned in and nipped

177

his ear lobe with her sharp teeth. "I swing both ways. Don't you, babe?"

Elijah pulled away but she would not be shaken so easily.

At that moment, the ship took the broad force of a giant wave on the port side. The shift seemed to unfold in slow motion as the ship tipped over. Glasses fell, bottles were broken. Excited cheers broke out among the group, sounding less certain moments later as the ship continued to angle to starboard. People lost their footing. Elijah and Shanitta grabbed the edge of the fixed banquette to stop themselves from falling.

The ship teetered at an angle. It seemed like forty-five, fifty degrees.

Jesus, Elijah thought, *this thing will go all the way.*

Images of *The Poseidon Adventure* ran through his mind.

What a way for this damn thing to end.

With a sudden snap, the ship jerked back to an upright position.

Relief was instant. Laughter and cheers broke out around the lounge. Some people began to clap.

He knew the ship could only go so far over before correcting itself, but just for a moment, Elijah had thought the worst.

At least it had shaken off Shanitta.

He hurried forward, still hunting for his friend.

When he rendezvoused with Helen and Orestis at the other side of the room, they were on their own.

"This storm is far worse than forecast," Helen said. "That was a close one."

Elijah took her elbow. "You need to face the fact that Anouska is probably not on board this vessel. And if she's out in the water, in that..."

Helen raised both hands to her head and suddenly looked twenty years older. "You're right. It's time to speak to the captain."

* * * *

Daniel and Terry burst into his stateroom seconds before the massive wave hit the ship.

Though it lasted only a moment, Daniel felt like time was frozen as he took in the scene.

The balcony door was open and a wind howled through the cabin, billowing the curtains. At the foot of his bed, Oliver squatted over a suitcase. His elbows were hooked into the armpits of a figure in the case as he tried to heave it out. Daniel blinked fast and looked again.

Good God, it's Anouska.

He saw straight away that she was dead. Her skin was a sickening shade of grayish blue. Her eyes were open and lifelessly unfocused. Her mouth gaped slackly.

He looked from her dead face to Oliver, who stared back at him, wide eyed and crazy.

"What have you done?" Daniel gasped.

Before Oliver could answer, the wave struck.

Suddenly the room tilted at an extraordinary angle. The contents of the dresser and night tables, anything that was not fixed down, spilled over. There was the sound of breaking glass as bottles hit the wall. Oliver dropped the corpse and fell face forward onto the suitcase. The case itself slid then rolled over, spilling Oliver and Anouska to the floor. They landed against the interior wall with a heavy thud.

Daniel tried to run toward them. It was like scaling an ever-inclining hill. He thought for one terrible moment that the ship was about to go over. Whatever Oliver had done wouldn't matter because they would all soon be dead, sinking to the bottom of the ocean. He would never see Elijah again. That was the most crippling thought.

Ballast and gravity drew the ship back to an upright position.

For a second of dazed relief, no one spoke or moved.

Daniel had stopped breathing during the roll and drew a great breath. *Panic over.* He had to keep it together. These ships were made to withstand the worst the ocean could throw at them. Let the captain worry about the conditions — he had his own problem right here.

Daniel raced across the room. Anouska was dead. He knew it with certainly, even before he touched her cold, stiff body. But he persisted, checking for signs of life. He lifted her flat onto her back and pressed his cheek against her mouth, his hand on her chest, just as he'd done with Vladislav. Nothing. She must have been dead some time.

"What did you give her? The same shit you used on Vlad?"

On his feet, Oliver had leapt to the other side of the bed. He stared wildly at Daniel then toward the door, hunting for a way out. Terry blocked the exit.

"You won't get past me, you bastard," Terry spat. "How is she? Daniel? Is she all right?"

"No," he cried, putting his hand on Anouska's cheek, as though he could still comfort her. "She's dead."

"Why?" Terry screamed at Oliver. "What did she ever do to you?"

"And what did you do to Vladislav?" Daniel said. "He's still got a chance. Tell us what you gave him and maybe the doctor can save him."

Oliver looked long and hard at Daniel. When he spoke, his voice was chillingly flat. "This all because of you. Vladislav wasn't supposed to take that drink. You were. And Anouska — she wouldn't be dead now if she minded her own business. I had nothing against either of them. I didn't like them, but I wouldn't have hurt them. Yes, it's your fault that they are where they are."

"He's mad," Terry said.

That much was obvious. Oliver was crazy. It might be a momentary thing, but there was nothing in the eyes glaring at Daniel except insanity. He'd intended to throw Anouska's body off the balcony. If they had arrived any later she would already be gone and they would never know what had happened. Except Oliver had gone to the trouble of bringing her to his room, so he obviously had a bigger plan in mind. To frame him? Or send him the same way?

"Tell me," Daniel said slowly, struggling to keep the anger from his voice. This cabin was a powder keg of fractious emotions, he didn't want to light the fuse. "Tell me that this isn't because of a few jobs you missed out on all those years ago. Tell me she's not dead for something as trivial as that."

"*Trivial*," Oliver choked and fat tears rolled down his face. "Trivial? Is that what you think it is? Trivial? You have taken everything that mattered from me since I was nineteen years old."

Daniel sighed, exasperated and sad. It *was* as bad as that. A young woman was dead and a man lay comatose because of a petty show business conflict. A rivalry that only existed in Oliver's twisted mind.

"You were sacked from Overload before I ever came along."

"No. I was the singer. The fucking lead. Till you screwed the manager and got him to sack me."

"That's not what happened. I auditioned for the band *after* you were fired. I didn't even know about you until later. Besides, what difference does it make? We were a flop. You said so yourself. It didn't do either of us any good."

"It wouldn't have been a flop with me," Oliver said. "It flopped because of *you*."

"Maybe it did, maybe it didn't. It's hardly important."

"Exactly," Terry said. "Jesus, kid, if I killed someone every time they beat me to a job, I'd have more deaths on my hands than Agatha Christie. It's show business. It goes with the territory. You pick yourself up and start again. You don't go on a killing spree."

"It wasn't just the boy band," Oliver snarled, spraying saliva across the room. "Every time I secured a career break, he was there. *The One*. I should have won that show but he saw to it that they kicked me out before it reached the public vote."

Oliver had a corrupt view of the history they shared

181

but Daniel didn't contradict him. Just let him rant if that was what he wanted. There was no time to listen. Daniel reached for the phone.

"*Put that down,*" Oliver screamed.

"We can talk about this as much as you want later," he said. "Right now, I'm calling the doctor so you can tell him what Vladislav has taken."

"Daniel," Terry said, "he's got a knife."

He looked up. Oliver stood across the bed from him, wielding a carving knife. Its twelve-inch blade glinted in the light and looked lethally sharp. "Put the damn phone down."

Daniel did as he asked, projecting the appearance of calm. Inside he felt icy fear. Oliver had already shown how dangerous he was and how far he would go. They had him cornered like a rat and he was capable of anything.

"Oliver," he said calmly. "This isn't right. You're not a bad person. You don't have to do this. Any of it. I have never intentionally done anything to hurt you. Those auditions, I was up against a lot of people. It was nothing personal against you."

Oliver shook his head. "You're here now, on this ship. I don't believe that's a coincidence. No fucking way it is. The big headliner with extra shows and a fancy stateroom while the rest of us slum it below. Why this ship anyway? Of all the ships at sea, you show up where I'm working. Expect me to believe you didn't plan that? You must take me for a right cunt." He waved the knife menacingly at Daniel.

It was spiraling out of control. Oliver was losing it fast. Daniel sought to keep his voice calm, unthreatening. "I've worked on a dozen or so ships this summer, all over the continent. I've got an agent in England who makes the bookings. I just go where I'm told. P&O, Cunard, Celebrity, Atlantic — I've been on all their European ships at one time or other. Some days I didn't even know where I was. I don't know who will be on any of the ships until I arrive. Nothing is planned, I promise you. When I arrived on the *Anthem* and saw you were here, I was delighted. At last, I thought, a chance to get to know Oliver. For all our paths have crossed, we've spent no time together. I thought this could be it."

"Bullshit! You stole my show."

"What show?"

"The Saturday matinee," Oliver hissed.

"Excuse me," Terry interrupted. "But *that* was my show. If anyone has the right to be pissed off it's me, but I'm not going around waving knives at people. Most of us are leaving tomorrow, no one gives a shit."

"Oh, shut up, you old has-been," Oliver said. "You've had your career. Count yourself lucky. I never made it because of this one here. I'd love to be a has-been because it would mean I was famous in the first place."

"Don't worry on that score, darling. You're about to become very famous, given your handiwork here. You'll be all over the news by this time tomorrow."

"Terry," Daniel advised, "that's not helping."

The ship gave another violent jerk to starboard as a second huge wave battered her side. Daniel was flung backward against the wall while Oliver fell across the bed, landing face down.

Daniel saw his chance and took it. Lunging for Oliver, he reached for the hand with the knife.

Oliver's reaction was too fast. He thrust back as the ship corrected itself and Daniel landed on an empty bed. Undeterred, Daniel followed. Pushing through his legs, he fired himself at Oliver's back, landing on his shoulders. They clashed against the dresser on the far side of the room. The wet, wind-torn curtains whipped across Daniel's face. He couldn't see but held on tight.

Oliver jabbed the knife backward, slashing at the weight on his back.

The blade slide across Daniel's left forearm, cutting so sharp and deep there was no pain at first. He would feel it later. Oliver drove an elbow into his stomach, winding him.

"Drop the knife," Daniel said, wrapping an arm around

Oliver's throat.

"Fuck you." Oliver jabbed his elbow back with greater force. He used the knife to tear at the arm around his throat, slicing another deep wound into the flesh of Daniel's forearm.

Daniel loosened his grip and dropped to the floor.

He staggered backward onto the balcony.

Grinning like a manic, Oliver followed, brandishing the bloodstained knife ahead of him.

Strong winds tore at Daniel's body. Rain and sea spray lashed across the balcony, making it slippery underfoot.

Oliver edged closer with the knife. "Now you will get what you deserve. You evil bastard. Twelve long years I've been waiting for this, now you're going to get it."

"No." Daniel raised his hands to deflect the knife but Oliver was fast.

The long blade slid into the soft flesh of Daniel's abdomen.

Above the howling sound of the wind, Terry heard the scream.

He flew around the bed. The ballooning curtains blocked his view of the balcony but he pushed on undeterred.

Oliver was mad beyond all reason. He had killed at least once today. He would have to kill Terry himself before he'd let him take another life.

Outside, Daniel was bent practically double, clasping his left side. Blood ran through his hands.

Oliver stood over him, lips twisted in a vicious snarl, teeth bared. The long knife raised to strike again.

"This is more satisfying than I imagined." His words carried into the room on the wind.

He took another step toward Daniel.

"No fucking way," Terry muttered to himself.

Moving with the kind of speed and strength he no longer thought he possessed, Terry reached onto the balcony and grabbed Daniel's shirtsleeve. He hauled him back into the room in a single superhuman action and slammed the sliding door shut. Daniel fell onto the bed, groaning. Terry locked the airtight door.

Oliver came at the door in a fury, banging fruitlessly with the handle of the knife.

"Let me in."

Terry had never seen such twisted evil and fury as that which flashed across Oliver's features.

"Throw the knife over the side," Terry shouted through the glass.

"Let me in, you stupid old bastard. I'll fucking kill you." Oliver was soaked from the rain and the sea. With his hair pasted to his head and water streaming across his angular features, he looked entirely feral.

"Throw the knife overboard," Terry shouted.

Oliver banged on the door with renewed fury.

Terry turned to the bed. Daniel had hunched into a ball. There was a lot of blood but he was still moving. Terry grabbed the first thing that came to hand, a T-shirt, and rolled it up. He had to stop the bleeding and get the doctor in here. He turned Daniel onto his back, opening his shirt. The cut was straight and deep, bleeding bright red. Terry put the T-shirt over the wound and pressed hard. Daniel groaned in pain but he kept the pressure on.

On the balcony, Oliver continued to pound on the glass. There was no way he could break it. He still had the knife, so he wasn't getting in. A new look came over his features — panic. He searched for a way in, working the handle, but it was sealed securely from the inside. He locked eyes with Terry through the glass. There was a new kind of madness in his gaze.

It would haunt Terry St. King for the rest of his life.

Oliver Gill turned away from the window and stepped to the edge of the balcony. Without glancing back, he mounted the rail and rocketed over the side into the furious Atlantic Ocean.

Terry snatched the telephone and dialed reception.

"Man overboard," he screamed.

Epilogue

Three weeks later

The funeral for Anouska Frost took place one drab Wednesday morning at the end of November. A raw and wet day with a northwesterly wind driving from the Irish Sea. But the weather couldn't discourage the crowd that gathered to pay their respects, nor the swarm of journalists, TV crews and cameramen who assembled outside the church in Salford where the service took place.

For three whole weeks, events on board the *Atlantic Anthem* had been front page news. Even the year's *Strictly* contestants were consigned to the lesser pages. The final voyage of the *Anthem's* maiden season was bigger news.

Alerted by the frantic chatter between ships and coastguards that fatal night, the press had been waiting in force at Southampton when the *Anthem* had docked six hours late on Sunday morning. While the search continued at sea for the body of Oliver Gill, gossip had leaked from the ship. Using the vessel's state of the art wi-fi, the news broke across the social media accounts of several passengers.

The singer Daniel Blake has been stabbed. One dancer is dead. Another lost at sea.

It was the story that had everything. Fame, envy, violence and revenge.

The public and the press lapped it up.

Anouska's funeral today would bring the story to its logical end. Every network and publication had someone at the church to snatch their share.

Several faces that had become familiar over the course

of the drama had already arrived and entered the church. Helen McDonald, cruise director, and Captain Roman Rassimov, commander of the *Anthem*, were among the first to turn up. There were other representatives from the massive cruise company but Helen and the captain were the most well-known. Helen wore a somber black trouser suit while Rassimov turned out in full naval uniform. They ignored the cameras and headed straight inside.

Vladislav Kolodin, another prominent and newsworthy figure in the story, arrived with a couple of dancers from the *Anthem* company. Cameras clicked and flashed. The handsome dancer had almost become the second victim of the psychotic Oliver Gill. While the drama had unfolded around him, Vladislav had lain unconscious, at death's door, having consumed the poisoned drink intended for Daniel. Vladislav glanced fleetingly at the press before heading into the church without comment.

The next big flurry of excitement came with the arrival of Terry St. King. Terry disembarked from the back of a long black limousine, stepping in front of the waiting photographers like a starlet attending her first premiere. He wore a long black coat and a black fedora with a magnificent feather in the brim. He smiled modestly and gifted them a royal wave.

Terry had become a big deal since the *Anthem*'s fateful return to Southampton. He was the hero of the story. The man who'd saved Daniel. Everyone wanted a piece of him and he was happy to give it. He had appeared on the BBC Breakfast show and the lunchtime news. He had bookings for *The One Show* that very evening and *Loose Women* the following afternoon. He'd grown into a self-titled icon, though no one could actually remember what he had ever been famous for.

'You know, he used to be on the telly. Years ago, on that thing. Oh, what was it called again?'

It was generally acknowledged that he must have been famous at some point. Most people, when asked, admitted that they had heard of him. They just didn't know where from.

"Such a very sad day," he announced to the reporters. "Anouska was such a dear, dear friend and a lovely girl. A beautiful life cut short."

"Did you attend Oliver Gill's funeral?" A question, yelled above the crowd.

Terry's narrow face stiffened. "No, I didn't. I feel sorry for his family, of course, but I have nothing in the way of condolence to give."

Oliver's cremation had taken place at a private ceremony in Blackpool the week before. The inquest into his death was scheduled for the beginning of January but the police investigation had already closed. They might never know what had driven him to do the things he did but there was no question regarding the cause of his own death — suicide.

There was another furor of excitement as the next black car pulled up. Elijah Mann climbed out of the back, followed moments later by Daniel Blake. Though the injuries Daniel sustained at the hands of Oliver had not been life threatening, he was still in some pain and stiff as he straightened up. The cameras flashed and the photographers jostled with each other for the best shot.

Elijah came toward them, hands raised. "Guys, please. C'mon, this is a funeral. A little respect for the family."

He walked back around the car and took his lover by the hand. Together they walked toward the church. It was an image that would feature on many of the next day's front pages.

Toward the edge of the crowd stood a lone figure. Dressed in black, somber faced, no one paid much attention to the quiet stranger. All eyes were focused on the church.

"Poor Daniel," someone said.

"He looks so frail," commented another.

"He'll get over it. He's a fighter. A survivor."

"He'll come back stronger than ever."

There were murmurs of agreement throughout the crowd.

Behind a large pair of shades, the stranger's eyes tightened, watching Daniel and Elijah as they walked into the church. The stranger's face remained fixed and emotionless.

No one nearby would suspect the anger and hatred that festered behind the calm façade.

Revenge shouldn't be rushed in the heat of such strong emotions. The stranger knew that.

Patience. Time.

Oliver would be avenged when Daniel and Elijah least expected it.

* * * *

"Feeling okay?"

"I'm fine."

"We shouldn't have stayed so late. You look tired."

"Stop fussing. I wanted to stick around. I needed to meet Anouska's family."

"Take a seat and I'll fetch you a drink."

Daniel sank onto the soft, oversized sofa in Elijah's living room. He slipped off his shoes, loosened his black tie and undid the top two buttons on his shirt. That felt better.

He was tired but it had nothing to do with his healing injuries. Funerals always took it out of him. Even worse when mourning the loss of someone so young.

The last three weeks had been a blur. Chaos. So many questions to answer. From the police, the crew, officials from Royal Atlantic, Anouska's family, Oliver's family. One day had merged seamlessly into another. It was only this week, when he'd visited the hospital and had his stitches removed, that he felt his life get back to some kind of normality.

Oliver was never far from his thoughts, day or night. What drives Oliver to do the things he does? The question might never be answered.

Even now, Daniel didn't know.

He examined the past, looking for any kind of clue. He dug out his dad's old recording of his appearances on *The One* and scoured through the episodes when he featured next to Oliver. There weren't that many. They had appeared on screen together twice, during one of the group auditions. Then there was the episode which cut Oliver from the competition. It was painful to watch. The very nature of TV talent shows made them a humiliating experience for the evictees and Oliver's was no different. But Daniel kept looking, re-watching the scenes of them together, hoping he would find some small clue in his own behavior that might have triggered Oliver's deadly obsession. There were none.

Elijah came back from the kitchen, bringing two glasses which tinkled with ice. He had taken off his suit jacket and his tie. He looked extraordinarily handsome in his open necked shirt.

"Vodka," he said. "Good and strong."

"Just what I need."

Daniel drank gratefully. Elijah sat beside him and put an arm around his shoulder.

That was where he had been for the last three weeks — by his side. And it was exactly where he needed him.

Daniel leaned into the crook of his arm, placing his head against his shoulder.

"Do you think we can get back to normal after this?"

Elijah kissed the top of his head. "I don't know what normal is anymore. Not since I met you. You've changed my whole world."

"Mine too. And despite all that's happened, that change is for the better."

It was the start of something new, something different, and they were in it together.

Daniel Blake and Elijah Mann.

Their song was just beginning.

Closer by Morning

Excerpt

Chapter One

Matt Blyth was not a morning man. When his alarm went off at five a.m. it shocked him awake. *What the hell?* Dragged rudely out of dreamland, where he'd been sailing across the Atlantic on a luxury cruise ship, to the darkness of his bedroom on Monday morning. Then he remembered the reason for the alarm. Boot camp. Today would be his first session. What had made him think that was a good idea?

He forced himself out of bed. *No time to think about this. Just do it.*

He stumbled to the bathroom and threw water in his face and raked wet fingers through his dark, wavy hair. Ten minutes later, dressed in joggers and running shoes, he was out of the house. He felt nauseated with the lack of sleep but pushed through it. Minor discomfort would not deter him, not when he was set on doing something he wanted.

He was twenty-eight years old. In a little over a year he would turn thirty, that first great milestone of age. He was determined to be in his best shape ever when the dreaded day came. Even if it meant getting up well before dawn to slog it out and sweat for an hour before work.

The morning, which felt like the dead of night, was damp and cold. The sky was still ink black as he steered his car off the estate and onto the road that would take him out of town. It wasn't far to the assembly point, a little over two miles. Soon, when he got used to these God-awful early rises, he wouldn't need the car, he would jog to the meeting place. But not yet. Not today.

Matt turned on the radio. Music usually got him going but the radio was tuned to a local station, just in time for the news. He let it play. He liked to know what was happening in the area, as well as getting the sports results and weather.

The lead item blasted away the final cobwebs of sleep.

"Durham Police have cordoned off an area of the river bank in the city following the discovery of a body late last night. Police refuse to speculate whether the death is connected to that of student Conner Welsh, whose body was discovered just two weeks ago downriver of the latest finding. Mr. Welsh was severely beaten before being strangled. Durham FM News will bring you further information on the latest death as we receive it."

Two bodies dragged from the river within a fortnight. That was unheard of in a small city like Durham. Murder of any kind was rare. He hoped the latest death was nothing more than an accident—a tragic coincidence—in no way connected to the murdered student. Drunk students had always been drawn to the riverbank. Too much alcohol and a loss of balance could have fatal consequences. From what he'd heard, Conner Welsh, the previous victim, suffered a nightmare ordeal before going in the water. He prayed it hadn't happened again.

The story continued to trouble him as he followed the winding country road, though he tuned out the rest of the bulletin and missed the sports update. The image of the murdered student had been a regular feature in the local press these last two weeks. A smiling, happy boy. Young and good-looking, a university student, Conner had everything to smile about. But some sick bastard had thought otherwise. Matt hoped they quickly found who was responsible, for the sake of Conner's family and the wider community.

Thin fingers of light began to crawl across the sky when he pulled into the car park at Binchester Woods. A handful of vehicles were already parked and a group of people in sports clothes were limbering up and stretching against the picnic table.

So there were others just as crazy as he was, coming out to exercise at this early hour.

There was no sign of Annabel's Fiat among the parked cars. Typical. This crazy venture was her idea. "C'mon, Matt," she had enthused in the office kitchen. "We'll motivate each other. And think how great it will be to get it over with so early in the day. No more having to drag our tired butts to the gym after work. Our evenings will be our own."

He had texted her the night before to make sure she was still up for the challenge.

Definitely she had replied and had added a smiley face.

Matt locked the car and headed toward the group of people. There were four men and three women, all of them swaddled in layers from head to foot.

"Is this the meeting point for boot camp?" he asked, certain it must be. Why would they be here otherwise?

A large man stepped forward. He carried a hardback notebook and a pencil. "It is. I'm Clint. I'm instructing the group today."

"Hi." They shook hands. "You spoke to my work colleague on the phone. Annabel Faith. She made the booking for both of us."

Clint consulted his little notebook. "Matt, is it?" He ticked him off his list. "Is your friend with you?"

"No. But she only has to come from town. She shouldn't be long." She had better not be.

Clint was huge. Exactly how Matt imagined a boot camp instructor would look—an enormous, ex-military, brick shithouse. With his steely crew cut and dark, hooded eyes, he looked like a hard case who would take no prisoners. He was sexy too, in a strange, scary way. Not really Matt's type, but he could see the appeal.

Clint enquired about his current level of fitness.

"Decent, I'd say. I train at the gym three or four times a week and like to run at weekends. I eat plenty of protein and take it easy with carbs. I'm just looking to improve my overall levels of fitness." All true, if slightly exaggerated.

Clint looked him over closely before making notes in his book. "Good. Any health concerns I should know about before you start?"

"None."

"Sure? This is an intense course."

"That's what I'm looking for. Something I can't get at the gym."

Clint nodded, satisfied, and closed his book. "You've come to the right group. Whipping bodies into shape, that's what I'm known for. No messing, no time wasting, no excuses—just exceptional results. A guy in my group last year made the front cover of *Men's Health* magazine. Those are the kind of results I aim for."

Matt stretched while they waited for the rest of the group to arrive. Clint told him they would leave at five-forty-five sharp. "Get here later than that and we'll be gone."

There was still no sign of Annabel. Punctuality wasn't one of her strong points. If she intended to turn up at all. Knowing her, she would still be curled beneath her duvet. He was mad for listening to her in the first place. She never came through, always full of enthusiastic ideas but with little success in achieving them.

More vehicles began to pile into the car park and soon there was a group of around twenty assembling for the class. They were mainly men, aged twenty through to mid-forties. Intense, serious-looking men who didn't mess about over fitness. Real go-hard-or-go-home types. Maybe it was a factor of the unsociable hour, but there wasn't much conversation going on. That suited Matt. Nobody wanted small talk at this time of day.

He cast an appraising eye over the group. They were fit, masculine, real men's men, but, a little bit like Clint, he found them rather asexual. Not his type at all. Not that he was looking anyway, but hey, a little eye candy could provide great motivation.

Just before the appointed start time another vehicle pulled into the car park and a man in blue running pants and a gray hoodie jumped out and jogged toward Clint. They spoke briefly and the instructor made a few hurried notes in his book.

Matt's interest was piqued by the new arrival. This was more like it. Even from a distance, he could see this guy was something very special. With short, dark blond hair and a light beard, he was as manly as the rest of the group but seemed to lack the focused intensity that made them so fearsome.

He even smiled as he left Clint to join the group. A lovely, winning smile that wrinkled the corners of his sparkly eyes and illuminated a broad, handsome face.

"Hi, guys," he addressed the group as a whole in a warm American accent.

"Hi," Matt replied while the others responded with a non-committal grunt or nod.

Unselfconsciously, the newcomer began to stretch.

Matt found it hard not to stare. Wow. This guy looked good from a distance but was even better close up. He had the broad build of a man in his thirties and, though he was swaddled in layers like the rest of them, Matt could discern the strong lines of his shoulders and butt through that clothing.

But it was his face, with its twinkly eyes and golden skin,

that was so exceptionally handsome.

Matt, with his wavy brown hair, brown eyes and angular face, was good-looking. He wasn't vain or conceited about it, he knew he was attractive, but couldn't help feeling inadequate beside the glorious American. With a face like that, he could do anything he wanted and the world would accept it—model, actor, politician, king.

Take it easy. Matt turned away. It was the only way to keep from staring.

He had the beginnings of an erection.

He'd wanted eye candy and now he had it. He'd have to be careful that the American didn't become a distraction rather than a motivation.

Clint Dexter's boot camp was advertised as the toughest, most effective workout in the county. *Hard work and effort get results!* proclaimed the poster in the window of his town center fitness studio. *Nobody trains you harder.*

It was no lie.

Without equipment, weights or gimmicks, Clint pushed his group on the most intense and physically grueling workout Matt had ever known. Clint was old school in his methods. Like an army sergeant breaking in the new recruits, he drove them uphill and into the woods. There was no let-up. He shouted and blew whistles, breaking up the run with demands for press-ups, squats, lunges, then straight back onto the track, going higher up the steep hill. There were no breaks. No moment to catch a breath.

Matt believed he was in good shape. Epic mistake. Every muscle in his body seemed to ache. His lungs were ablaze as he drew one arduous breath after another. *Shit.* He'd never known anything like this. And it didn't stop. For the whole hour Clint worked them hard—no slacking, no respite.

Matt was glad to see he wasn't the only one struggling with the course. He might be the newbie but even the seasoned old-timers were taking it badly. Everyone was red-faced and grimacing with pain.

Finally Clint guided them back down to the car park. It

was over.

"Make sure you all stretch down thoroughly," he shouted as he walked among the group. Most people were bent double, clutching their knees and gasping. "You'll pay for it later if you don't take the time now."

"Some group, eh?"

Matt realized that he was standing beside the handsome American. The course was so exhausting that he'd stopped paying attention to the blond hunk after the first five minutes. His hair was soaked, plastered to his head, and his face burned red, yet he exuded a sexiness that would have caught Matt's breath if he wasn't already wrecked.

Matt struggled to speak. "My first time," he gasped.

"Yeah? Me too. I thought I was fit until this morning. This guy has destroyed me."

"I doubt anyone is fit enough for this."

The American laughed. "You could be right. I've had personal trainers in the past. Let me tell you, none of them worked me half as hard as this dude. Not ever."

"Think you'll do it again?"

"Absolutely. A month of this and we could compete as Iron Men."

"You might be right. If we survive a month. My heart might not be able to take it."

"I'm Dale," he said. "Hi."

"Hello. I'm Matt."

"Nice to meet you, Matt," Dale said cheerily.

Matt was struck again by just how good-looking Dale was. God, his eyes – they were as blue as a cloudless August sky.

As he stretched his tired muscles, Matt tried not to be affected by the proximity of Dale, but it wasn't easy. It wasn't just the way he looked, it was his manner and the confidence he exuded. Even the smell of him, the sweat from all that hard work, was an aphrodisiac. It was a long time, if ever, since a man had had such a devastating effect on him. When Dale bent over to touch his toes and gave Matt the full benefit of his glorious rump, he had to turn away. Tenting the front of his pants with a hard-on was not the kind of first-day impression he wanted to make.

The sun finally put in an appearance, breaking weakly through the clouds above the jagged tree line.

"I've got to beat it," Dale said, straightening up and thrusting a hand at Matt. "Will you be here for the next session?"

Matt took his hand and was transfixed by those eyes. This must be how a rabbit feels as he's about to become road kill. "Wednesday? Yes, I'll be here." Truthfully, he hadn't been sure he had more than one early start a week in him, but that was before he met Dale. If he needed a reason to drag his tired butt out of bed, this was as good as he'd find.

"Great. I'm glad to see I'm not the only new guy. We're in this together now. Got to give those regular guys a run for their money, don't you think? So I'll see you Wednesday. Bye for now, Matt."

Dale jogged toward his car, giving Matt one final glimpse of his beautiful bouncing butt.

What was that? Matt felt as though he'd been picked up, spun around and dropped back down again. Had Dale been flirting? Or was that just American friendliness? Probably, Matt reasoned. He was so used to British reserve and surliness that he'd misread the signs. Dale was being friendly, that was all.

He shouldn't hope for more.

* * * *

Two hours later, showered, dressed and breakfasted, Matt walked through the doors of Benedict and Taylor, the long-established law firm where he'd worked since finishing college, ready to face the day. He *really* was ready. Despite the early start and punishing routine in the woods, he felt amazing. More energized for a Monday morning than anyone had a right to be. Maybe it was worth it and those people who worked out before the rest of the world had had their first cup of coffee weren't as crazy as he'd always thought. Exercise did have its benefits, besides meeting sexy strangers, and this early feeling of energy was a previously undiscovered one.

One look at Monica, sitting bleary-eyed on the reception desk, chugging from a bucket-sized carton of takeaway coffee, convinced him he was right.

"Rough night? Rough weekend? Year?" he asked.

"Very funny," she sneered, booting up the computer. "It's Monday, unless you've forgotten. Only freaks come in to work on Monday with a smile on their face."

"I'm smiling, aren't I?"

"Like I said – freaks!"

She sipped her coffee, looking him up and down. In his dark blue suit, pale shirt and narrow tie, clean shaven with his unruly hair combed into a neat style, he bore little resemblance to the wild creature who had stumbled out of bed all those hours before. Wearing a suit each day was part of the job and Matt Blyth wore it well. Six-foot-two with broad shoulders and a slender waist, he had the classic male physique that suits were designed for. The cheapest, off-the-rack two-piece still looked great on him.

"You *do* look unusually happy," Monica said, narrowing her eyes. "Why? Did you have a lottery win over the weekend? Or did you strike it lucky in other ways? A tumble in the sack?"

"It's the joy of life, Monica. You should try it sometime."

"Huh? You should try sitting here eight hours a day, five days a week and listen to people bitch because they can't get an appointment. See how joyful you feel then."

Matt's office was on the first floor of an imposing Victorian mid-link terrace in the heart of the old city. He bounded up the stairs, two at a time, to retrieve the planner from his desk. *This is ridiculous.* Surely he couldn't feel this good because of a little extra exercise. If so, he should have done it years ago.

Every morning from nine till nine-twenty Edward

Benedict, senior partner in the firm and Matt's direct boss, held a brief team meeting in the ground floor conference room. The aim was to assess any outstanding work, go through what had come in overnight and fix what everyone had to do that day.

Edward was at the head of the table when Matt entered. He was a well-built man in his mid-fifties, with thick gray hair and a broad, often red face. He regarded Matt with serious eyes over the top of his wire-framed glasses. With the table only two-thirds full, Matt was glad he wasn't the last to arrive.

"Morning," he greeted the room and took a seat beside Trish Coleman, the firm's bookkeeper. She had been with the practice almost as long as Edward.

"Have you heard?" Trish asked as he poured a glass of water from the jug on the table. "There's been another murder in town."

"I heard they had found a body. Have they confirmed it's murder?"

"Not officially. Not yet. But I've heard it from various sources already this morning. It looks *exactly* like the boy they found the other week. Same circumstances and everything."

"Shit. Poor kids. Have they ID'd the body?"

"Not that I know of." Trish Coleman, with contacts in most other law firms and within the police force itself, was the first person to find out everything. Whatever she said would be easy to dismiss as gossip but Trish had been right about so many things, so many times before, it was stupid not to listen. Gossip was her life. If she decided to change careers she would make an excellent journalist. Her contacts were outstanding. "There's something else," she said, relishing the power of her knowledge. "The first victim, Conner Welsh — what hasn't been released so far is that he was severely assaulted — sexually. Before and after death."

"My God."

"I know. Isn't it awful?" Her eyes were indecently excited. "There's potentially a serial killer. A *sexual* serial killer. On the loose, right here in Durham."

"That's all idle speculation," Edward said firmly. He'd never approved of Trish's gossiping. Gossip worked both ways and he was suspicious of any information about the firm she might share with a rival in return for tittle-tattle.

For Matt, the shine was taken from his previous good mood. The discovery of another corpse was bad enough without the prospect of a sexual predator stalking the city. Unlike his boss, he was inclined to believe what Trish said. She was rarely wrong. The police needed to move quickly on the case before anyone else was killed.

Annabel Faith was the next to arrive. Edward glanced frostily at his watch as she came in, but it was not yet nine o'clock. Annabel had joined Benedict and Taylor six months after Matt and had been his best friend in the practice since her first day. There was less than a year between their ages and Annabel was like the young sister he had never had.

In a black trouser suit and silk blouse, Annabel had clearly spent some considerable time getting ready that morning. Her makeup was immaculate and her soft blonde hair had been straightened into a sharp style. Matt looked her up and down.

"So what's your excuse? Hair dryer emergency?"

"Sorry, sweetie, but I just couldn't face it. Not this morning."

"Neither could I but I still made the effort. It's what we agreed after all. You could at least have sent a text and told me you weren't coming."

"I didn't think you'd have your phone on you." She helped herself to a breakfast muffin from the pile on the table and sat beside him. "I said I was sorry, sweetie."

"I told them you would definitely be there," he lied. "The instructor was really pissed. The entire group waited for you."

Her mouth widened, as she was about to take a bite. "Oh

my God. Really? Were they mad? What did they say about me?"

Edward called the meeting to order. Not everyone was there yet, but a bit like Clint Dexter, he was a sucker for punctuality and starting on time. Matt decided to keep quiet for a while. It would do Annabel good to stew a little.

As usual, Edward went around the table, getting his staff to read out one by one what they had listed in their diaries for the day. It was the standard list of mundane matters, the kind of work that kept modest firms like this one ticking over.

"I've got two clients at court this morning," Matt said when it came his turn. "Magistrate's stuff over at Newton Aycliffe. One breach of the peace and one driving offense. Both are pleading guilty so it shouldn't take more than an hour. I was going to spend the rest of the morning preparing a trial I have tomorrow."

"Which trial?" Edward observed him over the rim of his glasses.

"Newby versus Lewis. A family matter. Dad is going for access rights to his son."

"Difficult?"

"Mother is being difficult but I think we can win. Her main argument against our client getting access is that he has a new girlfriend. Nothing to do with his suitability to have the boy. If I can get that across to the judge, I think I can get our client what he wants."

"Good. And this afternoon?"

"Appointments every half hour until six. Two new cases. It's a full schedule. And I'm on call tonight. This morning is the only time I have to prep the trial," he added hastily. Edward had a habit of spotting what he perceived to be gaps in his workers' schedules and filling them, with little consideration for the amount of work required before and after even the most mundane case.

"That's fine. Annabel?"

Less prepared, Annabel blustered through a sparse

calendar and tried to make herself sound busy. In reality she had little going on that morning, other than a few follow-up phone calls, and only appointments booked for the afternoon. Edward saw straight through the ruse.

"Take the files from Matt for the magistrate's cases. You can handle the sentencing. Matt, take the morning to prepare your trial for tomorrow. I think you'll need it."

"Thank you, sir. It's appreciated."

"You bloody crawler," Annabel said afterward, coming to Matt's office to collect the files she needed for court.

He laughed. "I didn't ask for this. The boss saw right through that crap you gave him. You've got bugger all to do today."

"I like to keep things light on Monday, you know that."

"So does Edward, *that's* your problem."

She pulled up a chair and sat, leafing through the files without taking much notice of what was inside. It was routine stuff. Nothing she couldn't deal with on the fly at court. "So how did it go this morning? Were they really pissed I wasn't there?"

"You'd love that, wouldn't you? But no, they weren't pissed. Nobody noticed to be honest, except me. This guy Clint, he doesn't wait around for people. If you're not there on time, too bad."

She flicked her hair across her shoulder. "What's he like? The instructor? A hottie or nottie?"

Annabel was a serial fiancée who had recently broke off her latest engagement. She was back on the market and finding a new man was her number one priority.

"He's okay. He's very fit but probably not your type."

"Hmmm. How old?"

"Fortyish. Thereabouts. It's sometimes hard to tell with those really muscular men. Too much muscle can be ageing. He might not be as old as all that."

"I need to find out for myself."

"Then you need to get your butt out of bed on Wednesday and be there at five-forty-five."

"You're going back?"

"I am. Unlike you, when I commit to something I see it through."

He decided not to tell her about Dale. Not yet. Selfishly, he hoped Annabel wouldn't show on Wednesday. He wanted the American to himself. At least until he had time to figure him out. The more he thought about him, the more convinced he became that Dale had been showing definite signs of interest this morning. Crazy, for sure, but Dale was so goddamn beautiful, he couldn't pass up the opportunity of seeing him again.

Even if it was just a sweaty yomp around the woods. When a man looked as good as he did, a moment of his time was better than nothing.

More books from
Pride Publishing

A trust destroyed is a trust that is hard to recover…

Nature versus nurture. Which one is the culprit?

John's said no in the past, but now he has a chance at
forever – if he can move past his doubts and say yes.

Part of the Totally 5 Star collection

*Sex, weddings and gambling hold a back seat to kidnapping
and murder in the city of sin…*

About the Author

Thom Collins

Thom Collins is the author of Closer by Morning, with Pride Publishing. His love of page turning thrillers began at an early age when his mother caught him reading the latest Jackie Collins book and promptly confiscated it, sparking a life-long love of raunchy novels.

Thom has lived in the North East of England his whole life. He grew up in Northumberland and now lives in County Durham with his husband and two cats. He loves all kinds of genre fiction, especially bonkbusters, thrillers, romance and horror. He is also a cookery book addict with far too many titles cluttering his shelves. When not writing he can be found in the kitchen trying out new recipes. He's a keen traveler but with a fear of flying that gets worse with age, but since taking his first cruise in 2013 he realized that sailing is the way to go.

Thom Collins loves to hear from readers. You can find contact information, website details and an author profile page at https://www.pride-publishing.com/